Rage grows in the soil of grief.
My heart pounds with torment.
Confronting heaven, I roar,
"Lord God! Do you hear me?
How could you allow
a cursed goat to kill my baby?
Oh, how can you even know
what I am suffering?
**Will you ever have to know
what it is to watch
a beloved son cruelly die?"**

MARAH

THE WOMAN AT THE WELL

Nina Mason Bergman

LIVING BOOKS
Tyndale House Publishers, Inc.
Wheaton, Illinois

To J O H N
My Beloved Husband Friend Teacher

ACKNOWLEDGMENTS

Thank you is one of my favorite statements.
For it implies that someone has seen a want
in my life and cared enough to meet that
need. It is to those certain friends, who
helped me through the writing of *Marah*,
that I wish to say thank you.

First to my husband, John, for his faithful
praising of every step I fearfully took in this
venture. I am grateful for the input of the
Mt. Hermon Writer's Conference. I recognize,
with appreciation, the special critique work
of Charles Repenning. To our critique group:
Alice, Marjorie, Dorothy, Andrea, and Ethel,
I will always be grateful.

In no way could or would *Marah* ever have
been completed without the expertise of
Ethel Herr. I am most indebted for her
teaching, guidance, and encouragement.

To you friends, thank you.

Second printing, November 1983
Library of Congress Catalog Card Number 82-62070
ISBN 0-8423-4032-7, paper
Copyright © 1983 by Nina Mason Bergman
Printed in the United States of America

INTRODUCTION

Jesus had a talk with a woman at a well.

The account is found in John, chapter four. In this passage we learn the woman was a Samaritan, married five times, and living with a man not her husband. We also find an intelligent woman, knowledgeable in both Samaritan and Jewish beliefs. She was open minded, looking for truth, aware of her need.

It is popular to cast questionable looks at her. *"After all, five husbands and a lover are a bit much, even for today!"* *"Did she not come to the well at noon, rather than at the customary evening hour, to avoid the scornful stares of other women?"*

We know of her many marriages and of her lover and often judge her—but did the townspeople of Sychar know?

It is easy to imagine any number of emergencies that might require a midday drawing of water, so it may not be fair to say she came at that hour because she lived in shame. Again, did her neighbors know of her life?

When Jesus confronted this Samaritan woman

with her five husbands and present lover, she was stunned. So stunned, in fact, that she accused him of being a prophet . . . even the Messiah!

I believe this woman's five marriages and lover to be her most private knowledge. Otherwise why such astonishment that Jesus knew? And if the gossips of Sychar were aware of her story, why should they care to walk all the way to Jacob's well to see a man who only that day had come upon such common news? Further, if her doings were familiar, then why be surprised that a Jew had also heard the gossip?

If, however, this woman's many husbands and lover were *her* secret, then utter shock would be in order when Jesus confronted her with the truth of her life.

After speaking with Jesus the woman rushed back to town, wild to share her discovery with the townspeople. "Come, see a man. . . ." The folk of Sychar must not have viewed her as a fallen woman, for they listened to her words and left to see Jesus. On just her testimony, they believed him to be the Savior of the world. Is this the response of a community to a woman who dares not come to the well when other women are present? I don't think so. She held their respect. They accepted her words; they followed her "Come." And afterward they discussed with her their own acceptance of her findings.

The story of this woman is fact, based on the witness of John.

The story of *Marah* is my imagination of who this woman might have been.

*Then Moses led Israel onward from the Red Sea,
and they went into the wilderness of Shur; they went
three days in the wilderness and found no water.
When they came to Marah, they could not drink
the water of Marah because it was bitter: therefore
it was named Marah. And the people murmured
against Moses, saying, "What shall we drink?"
And he cried to the Lord and the Lord showed
him a tree, and he threw it into the water, and
the water became sweet.* Exodus 15:22–25a (RSV)

ONE

"Eleazor?"

No response. Again I whisper a summons to the sprawled man slumbering by my side, "Eleazor?"

Of late my husband needs extra sleep. I try not to worry about his health, rather reason it must be his age which begs for additional rest.

I gaze upon his turned head and ache to muss the gray-black hair, knowing fully our game . . . low growls, followed by playful hugs, tender words, and at last fourteen kisses (one for each year of my life). But mindful of his need, I move silently from our bed.

In the gathering room I find slanted rays of the morning sun rearranging the room's shadows. The rich furnishings, however, remain exactly where Eleazor first placed them. Upon the pale walls hang the multi-hued rugs from Persia. The broad ebony table is neatly ringed by several

9

cushions. Our treasured brass urn reflects dawn's greeting. What could possibly undo this, our secure life? I am content.

And thirsty.

The water in the large jar almost touches the brim. I dip my cup and drink deeply. Wrapping a towel about my waist I next fill the wash basin. Although the water holds the night's chill, I bathe leisurely, shivering. After donning my newest dress I brush the tangles from my long, dark hair. Eleazor appreciates the care I give my appearance. As far back as memory stretches I hear his boast, "Marah is the fairest of all."

"Bless him," I sigh, smoothing a few fly-away hairs.

I push aside my apprehensions concerning Eleazor's health and step outside. There I inhale the soft air and am refreshed by its sweetness. Yellow sunlight outlines the lone date palm guarding our doorway. I see a cluster of poppies—they sleep wrapped in the tree's shade. In the distance a peacock screams news of morning's arrival, mindless it has been announced earlier by a neighboring rooster.

How wonderful are these choice moments, unique to day's opening, holding no demands, only promises. I am part of this drama. I, too, share in getting life underway as I coax the fire to dance, the fire that will cook our breakfast.

Eleazor is a man of habit. Every morning he must have little cakes topped with honey. Most successful merchants of Sebaste provide servants for household duties. But I choose to serve

Eleazor alone and care for his needs. He is my dear husband and his comforts I attend with delight. For him I mold the dough to the prescribed size while waiting for the flames to become embers. Meanwhile, daydreaming of the past, I stand near the warmth and muse.

Eleazor and my father, Jahath, companions in boyhood, remained friends even as men. Both became merchants. Eleazor, the committed businessman, never married. "Whatever would I do with a wife?" And that settled that.

I laugh, for now he daily queries, "Whatever would I do *without* a wife?"

At last the coals are ready. The little cakes send fragrant hints of a soon feast. The tempting aroma causes recollection of the many meals Eleazor ate at the table of my parents, reviewing news of the marketplace with Father and praising Mother's well-managed household. Mother, blushing, would routinely insist, "Eleazor, handsome as you are, I find you much too thin. Our servants are under orders to fatten up those bones!"

I grew up adoring this tall, happy man. Eleazor's peppered beard frames a mouth quick to widen in a smile. His laughter yet reminds me of a waterfall splashing in thundering joy. I think upon that laughter of Eleazor's. Once, during dreadful illness, it served me as medicine.

Two years have passed since that epidemic struck our land. It reached us at the beginning only by rumor. Then as a wild beast seizing its prey, the sickness struck with savage sudden-

11

ness, attacking my parents. Both were dead within a week's time. For many days I, too, lay sick, too stunned to mourn.

But Eleazor came, encouraging me back to life, nurturing me back to health. His kindness, caring, and wonderful laughter dissipated my self-pity and brought healing. Together we struggled with shared grief. He also suffered the loss, having long loved my parents.

Neither of us can recall how or when, but our relationship expanded. One day we recognized a compelling need for each other. I, in beginning womanhood, faced a future without direction or protection. Eleazor saw the approach of a lonely old age. We married. Moments now come, so enchanting that even a sigh is unuttered lest I return to childhood and Eleazor become once again an aging man.

Finished with my musings, I turn my attention to the golden brown cakes. A honey topping completes their appeal and honors my husband's breakfast habit. Eleazor has slept a good deal longer than usual.

"Eleazor! The songbirds, morning sun, and sweetcakes await you." I smile, recalling how comical he looks yawning.

"Eleazor! Come soon!" I urge, brushing aside a fly intruding upon our breakfast.

"ELEAZOR!"

Eleazor does not come. I find him, yet in bed, a soft look of peace upon his face. Cupping his knobby fingers to my cheek I groan, "Oh, my sweet Eleazor!"

A voice more demanding than mine has called. Eleazor's hand lies motionless in my grasp. I watch my tears fall into his palm and begin the routine washing of the dead.

TWO

Loneliness is a dreary companion. In the weeks following Eleazor's death I try fleeing its presence. I rise early and wander for hours, hoping to be rid of it, yet with each step the morose company follows.

This evening I sprawl upon the largest cushion that had been Eleazor's favorite place to think, for now I, too, must think. So many questions fill my mind, yet true to my upbringing, I dare not challenge the wisdom of God. But I do wonder what is to become of me. How am I to pass my days? What is to fill this void? Drained of feeling, I sit staring at a small square box on the ivory table in the corner by the door. Long ago this lovely box helped me through a great need. I pick it up and remember its magic.

My first tooth had fallen from my mouth, only to be followed a short time later by another. No one had ever told me this was routine in childhood. At play shortly thereafter, I learned the dreadful prognosis. Some big boys, bored with their games, found a new sport in my gullibility.

"It usually begins with the teeth," the tall one informed me.

"Terrible when it happens to a little kid," volunteered another.

One boy with a crooked nose glared hard at me. "Your fingers will probably be the next to go."

Their descriptive and gory arguments convinced me that, bit by bit, I was coming apart. I ran screaming for home, scarcely noting that the boys rolled with laughter. I hid behind a chest, waiting to disappear altogether. Father came upon his sobbing daughter and gently coaxed out the story of my dismal future.

"Look, my toes are loose," I bawled, wiggling them as proof. "Soon *all* my teeth will be gone and then my tongue will fall out!" The thought terrified me.

Father murmured reassurances. Patting my head, he explained he must be gone on a brief errand and I must be brave in his absence.

I tried to be calm, but fear possessed my soul. How many people did this happen to? I recalled the blind and limbless beggars of the marketplace. Panicked by the review, I took repeated inventory of hands, feet, and face. So far I was intact.

Father returned sooner than I had dared hope. "Come here, little Marah, I have a special gift for you."

Probably string, I reasoned, *to tie me together.* As I approached Father, I caught sight of a box

15

partially hidden by his large hands. I climbed upon his knee that I might have a better view. The box, of a dark brown wood, was carefully inlaid with ivory. Around the creamy white bulged pieces of colored glass. The sun's light streaming through the doorway touched the glass, filling the room with dancing spots of color.

Father smiled, yet his voice spoke with soberness, "My little daughter, this is a very special box. Not only will it hold your favorite items, but anything that falls off you and is put in this box will be replaced."

I studied the kind face of Father, the lovely box, then touched the empty place in my mouth with the tip of my tongue. Excitedly I ran to the bowl where two small teeth lay hidden. Father opened the box and I dropped the teeth trustingly into the darkness.

"There, now," he promised, "you will soon grow new teeth, even bigger than these."

Sure enough, in a few weeks new and larger teeth replaced the fallen ones. Broken fingernails put in the box were just as certainly replaced. The dreadful threats of the big boys lost their power. I owned a magical box.

Now, years later, I know greater loss. Eleazor is dead. Can the charm and power of my beautiful box undo death's work? No, nothing, no one, rules this foe. Pushing back the threatening onrush of grief, I rise to my feet knowing that tomorrow must hold more than a futile flight from sorrow.

But how? Where? And with whom?

Kinsmen, cousins of Father, live in the green hills outside of town. In past times when they brought goats to sell at the marketplace of Sebaste, they would call on us. We rarely visited at their farm, as Mother's frail health limited our outings. Not since Father's death two years ago have they come. Perhaps I should go there. At least it would be a start out of my solitary gloom.

Determined to escape this state of dreariness, I return my box to the small table and anticipate morning.

The marketplace is loudly alive with merchants and buyers, each insisting his price to be the fair amount. Obeying my new resolve, I join the pushing until I spot her, old Abigail, the hawker of anything that can be sold. This day she is selling fish. I try not to breathe too deeply.

"Good morning, Abigail."

"Well, hello yourself, Marah. Want some fish? Nice and fresh."

I retreat from the fish she waves. "Not today, thank you. But I do need your help. I wish to visit my father's cousin, Nabod. It has been a long while since I've traveled to his home. Can you tell me how to get there?" I remember my father telling me that Abigail knows everything about everybody.

Abigail's hands are dirty and crusted with fish scales. Nevertheless she slaps them to her face, exclaiming, "Well, of course, child! Can't forget a fat man who sells goats."

I fail to understand the connection. But then I never have been able to comprehend this woman who surely never washes and always wears layers of soiled clothing. Braving the added stench of her silvery wares, I try again. "Do you know where Nabod lives?"

This time she thumps her hips. "Of course, child, of course!" She pauses and peers intently at me. "Day after tomorrow I am going to the coast for . . . beads." She laughs, revealing her one comely feature, even, white teeth. "Nabod's house is on my way. Be here at daybreak and I will take you there."

I had not meant to visit quite this soon nor travel with this woman . . . until I see Abigail's piercing eyes.

"Day after tomorrow will be just fine."

"There it is!" Abigail shrieks, jerking me into position to see the sprawled, simple dwelling.

"Nabod takes his flock to the slopes, yet always a few goats mosey about the house. That Nabod is a strange one, he is."

I hold my own idea of a strange person to myself. To her I merely say, "You have been kind, Abigail. Thank you for bringing me here."

She touches my cheek with a dirty finger. "Marah, I am sorry that you are a widow while still a little girl. I liked your parents and skinny Eleazor. They were good ones, yes, they were good ones."

Turning her face from me, Abigail squints into the bright sun and starts to say more. I feel she wishes to speak tenderly. Instead she pulls her filthy, frizzed hair out further and mutters a quick good-bye.

I watch her march away. Eleazor and my parents sometimes spoke of "crazy Abigail" and laughed. At other times, it seemed to me, their voices lowered, almost with awe, when discussing her.

The nearby bleating of a small goat brings my attention to the house of Nabod. Abigail is right; goats indeed abound. And children. Suddenly I find myself besieged with boys and girls and questions. A round, red woman pops out of the doorway, smacking her hands together, ordering children to scatter and challenging me to account for my presence.

"Anna, I am Marah, daughter of Jahath, your husband's kinsman."

She squeals, leaps, and encircles me to her rotund body. I feel I am being swallowed.

"Oh, Marah, Marah, we heard that only a few months after the death of your poor parents you married Eleazor, and that now he too is dead. Come in, dear, and tell me about everything."

It is hard to stand while being hugged by a sphere. Regaining balance and poise, I follow my sweet kinswoman into her domain.

Everything is, at once, surprisingly clean and unbelievably cluttered. Anna clears a small bench and sets me there. The satchel I carry catches her attention.

"What did you bring with you? Lunch?"

Without waiting to be answered, Anna lifts my bag and replaces it with a bowl filled with chunks of cheese. Smiling, she watches as I eat a morning "lunch."

For hours we chat, sharing our news and hearts. It feels good to be mothered again. I almost forget my loneliness.

Nabod arrives before evening. I note he is as plump as Anna, and no taller. He arranges himself upon the largest goat-hair cushion, coughs into a fist, and begins a study of my every feature. Outside, the children amuse themselves with races, shouts, and laughter. Nabod pays no mind, his every attention is upon me. Finished with his findings, Nabod repositions his bulk, clears his throat, and announces, "Marah, we welcome you to our poor home. Do be comfortable here and enjoy our hospitality." His brief speech said, he pauses for my response.

"You are gracious, cousin Nabod. Already I have been welcomed with great kindness."

Nabod almost smiles, then unexpectedly a frown crosses his round face. "Marah, why did you not come to us following the death of your parents? We invited you, remember?" He taps the tips of his fingers together without making a sound.

"Cousin Nabod," I explain, "I was extremely ill. I couldn't even leave my bed. The fever and illness so weakened me I scarcely could move. Why, if it hadn't been for Eleazor's care I surely would have died!" Tears threaten to punctuate my words.

The loud clearing of Nabod's throat alerts me—another speech is forthcoming. His face reddens and the finger-tapping accelerates.

"You should not have married Eleazor! That was wrong, very wrong indeed."

A deluge of tears is on the way and I feel no compulsion to restrain them. "Wrong?" I wail, recalling my dear husband. "How could marriage to a man as fine as Eleazor be anything but right?"

Nabod locks his brow into a heavy scowl. Intimidated, I begin to tremble. Anna bounces to my side and wraps her ample arms protectively about me.

"Nabod!" she protests, "why do you scold the child?"

Unable to handle his wife's accusing words, Nabod paces. My tears also trouble him. Eventually he moves to my side and gently pats my hand while I recompose.

Again he speaks, this time with softer voice.

"With both your parents dead, I do understand your need to marry. Eleazor was certainly a splendid gentleman and a good friend to my late cousin. But, child! *He was not your kinsman!* You are a Samaritan woman. You must marry only a kinsman. Surely you know that."

Speechless and without defense I stare at Nabod. He is right. Duty demands marriage to a kinsman.

"Cousin," I sob, wiping my nose, "I am only fourteen, a widow, with no one to advise me. Please tell me what I should do."

Nabod coughs and ceremoniously rubs his bulbous nose. I prepare for whatever wisdom he is about to impart.

"Heber, my eldest son, is nearing eighteen. You would be a fine wife for him. Even now he needs help with his growing herds. Goats need tending."

The herds? Vaguely I recall playing with some goats on a long-ago visit. Somehow I never considered that they needed care. But Heber? Vaguer yet is my memory of him. My curiosity will have to be frustrated a while longer. This night Heber is out in the fields tending goats.

THREE

"Goats are intelligent animals," explains Heber, my husband of three weeks. "They can be fine companions." I look at the mass of bleating creatures and doubt his words. What I do believe is that every goat bred since Noah unloaded the ark belongs to Heber.

"Look over these slopes." Heber spreads his arms. "Do you see how my herds have multiplied from just a few goats?"

I nod, dismissing this news. Dutifully I have married my kinsman, dutifully I join him in the care of the herds, but I do not have to fill my head with goat-thoughts.

I determine to make this marriage of obligation as pleasant as possible. As I see it, the union is between Heber and myself. These beasts are not a part of the contract.

I turn my attention to Heber's face. Heavy, dark fuzz outlines the promise of a beard. His skin is tanned from living beneath the sun. Gratefully I decide he is much better looking than either Nabod or Anna.

Sensing my focus is drifting from goat education, Heber tugs at my hand and leads me to a young kid. The animal greets him with a gentle butting. Heber squats and roughs the nobs atop its head. "A man is fortunate who owns goats."

We wander among clusters of the grazing forms. "It is the breeding season, Marah, so I will spare you the meeting of the bucks."

"Oh, are they dangerous at this time?" I ask, moved that he has thought of my safety.

"No, my wife," Heber chuckles, tweaking his nose, "they stink."

Romance must be nonexistent in a goatherd, I decide.

The sun is warm and owns the heavens. We heed the lure of outstretched branches belonging to an aged tree, and recline upon the grasses in its lacy shade. I yearn to discuss the day's loveliness, Heber's childhood, or anything not to do with goats. But before me sprawls a man with one tune. He continues the recital exciting only to him. "The doe may be bred after she reaches eight months. Then 145 to 155 days later the offspring appear. Usually she will produce twins, but I have a few who have borne as many as four."

I force a smile and toss a fallen leaf at Heber. He catches it in mid-flight and holds it skyward. The leaf hovers a hand's span above the blowing mouth of my husband. Heber cheers his skill and the leaf plunges to the ground. We laugh until both of us are spent. Surely all goat talk is finished.

Heber's dark eyes meet mine. The corners of his narrow lips bend upward. His voice is low, edged in obvious tenderness.

"Did you know," he begins, smoothing the grass that I may move nearer, "did you know that a newborn kid can stand and run about right after birth? They are most appealing. I know you will want to hold every one."

I have no wish to embrace a goat of any age, rather I am filled with a longing to caress the soft petals blooming in the flower gardens of Sebaste. I keep these thoughts to myself, however, as anything I say only reminds Heber of some goat story.

I am as full of goat facts as I ever care to be, but no doubt Heber will find more such information to impart. Resigned to this fate, I drop my head upon his shoulder. The dips and rolls of the green expanse, the bright blue of cloudless sky, even the discordant melodies of the goats lull me into heavy drowsiness and daydreaming.

Suddenly angry shouts trespass into my world of reverie. Heber starts and then sits motionless. Less than a stone's throw away, four Roman soldiers, helmets aflame in noon's brightness, are bullying a hapless peasant. Apparently while carrying cloaks for the soldiers, the man stumbled. Heber and I watch in crouched silence.

"You stupid Samaritan!" screams the enraged Roman. "Can't you carry a small armful without falling? Even a donkey can manage a load and not trip over his own feet!"

I tremble as the Samaritan straightens to full

height, fists clenching while blue veins grow full on tense arms. His accusing eyes seek out and fasten upon this loud tormentor. I can see that deep within the man fierce indignation waxes and begs for release. If our countryman heeds these inner demands, the swords of Rome will strike. I gasp as his face contorts and pales, and expression vanishes. The Samaritan knows the system, Hail Caesar or be broken. He falls prostrate before the waiting quartet and pleads forgiveness for such clumsiness. Rome forgives, but first the peasant must learn his place. Sickened, I watch the kicking and hear the cries.

"Dog!" The leader orders. "Pick up our cloaks and come."

Dazed, bloodied, and humiliated, the man gathers his load and trudges behind these rulers of his world. The greater burden he carries within.

Almost without breathing, we watch the Samaritan and soldiers until we can see them no more. The presence of the happening lingers as a foul stench.

This is not the first time I have witnessed the harsh authority of our Roman peace. I recall my father's explanation. "The clouds rove the heavens, the sun warms the earth, the stars mark time, and the wind moves where it will. Caesar has no authority over these. But we who know clouds, sun, stars, and wind are of the land. This is Caesar's sphere. To him we must bow. But we wait. Messiah comes."

FOUR

Perched stair-step fashion on the weathered bench just outside the door, the young offspring of Nabod sit without a stir. Anna patrols the brood with all the authority of a Roman centurion.

"Children," she begins, waving her plump arms, "in a few moments we will be leaving for a day at the market." She stops her speech to inspect each child for cleanliness. "Many people will be there. It would be very easy to become separated from each other.

"Don't."

Enlightened by their mother's one-word command, the children now heed the smack of her hands and line up. They have already figured out that obedience to this woman and a long life go together.

Excitement races through me. I have not visited my Sebaste in all the months I've been

Heber's wife. As we start the long walk, I want to race. However, for the sake of the smallest children, we march slowly along. Nabod benevolently passes out coins to each youngster. Tight fists guard the new wealth, while without a doubt minds hold dreams of the wondrous marketplace.

From the onset, we can see the hill. Towering over the countryside is the city, once called Samaria, now Sebaste, as Herod renamed it in honor of Augustus Caesar.

As a small girl I often imagined myself queen, reigning over this fair land. What elegant robes I envisioned for my royal self. What wise rule I schemed for my realm. Sometimes I marched to the city's crest where I could spot any advancing enemy and alert my army of the threat. If the day were clear I could glimpse the distant blue waters of the Great Sea. Someday, I vowed, I would stand upon their shores.

Often my father recited the city's history to me. He felt pride in much of what Sebaste once was and had become. How I wish he were yet alive! Grief for Father, Mother, and Eleazor sweeps over me anew.

I force myself to think upon the ancient walls which once guarded the ivory palace. Masons from Phoenicia built these ancient structures nine centuries ago. Their enduring strength rallies my sagging spirit. How beautiful is this city we near. Only the presence of the Roman troops mars the graceful loveliness of the streets.

Father schooled me in the long-ago fall of all of Israel, of that lengthy exile, of the Jews who returned to Jerusalem and built a temple. He explained to me that during the exile many were held captive in Samaria. It is from these people we come. "We, too," he had said, "believe we are chosen of God. We do not worship in Jerusalem, but rather from the holy mountain, Mt. Gerizim."

"Father," I remember asking, "is that why the Jews don't like us?"

"In part, child. During the years of captivity people from other lands also were enslaved with us. Eventually there was much intermarriage. The Jews call us half-breeds and dogs, and look down upon us. In fact," he chuckled, "they think our bread turns into pork."

"Are we dogs, Father?" I began to cry.

"Of course not. We follow the law of Moses and look forward to Messiah. Someday he will come and all things will be made right. You are not a dog, my little daughter. God made you and he made you quite beautiful."

My musings fade as we at last walk through the gates of Sebaste. The streets are filled with the usual sounds of the city. The sights and aromas of the marketplace renew many feelings. We near the stall where cakes, rich with spices, are baking.

"Mama, I'm hungry!" wails the youngest. The others quickly join in the chorus claiming imminent starvation. Nabod protests, but buys a treat for all.

Anna's mission is to outfit each child and herself, since she doesn't do her own sewing.

This she wishes to do without interference from Nabod or me.

"Marah, why don't you go and enjoy yourself for a couple of hours. Nabod, you go tend to your business. The children and I need to shop. Meet at this booth when the sun is directly overhead."

When Anna makes a suggestion, it is actually a decree. I am happy to have the time alone.

By habit my feet take me to the house Eleazor and I shared. Once there, I stand and study every detail. Although tears blur my vision, I see the flowers by the palm are yet blooming. Near the doorpost stands the stone *mesusah,* typical of Samaritan homes. I can still see Eleazor as he placed it there. Touching it, he had whispered, "The law of God."

Today others own this home and reside in its lovely rooms. Besieged by memories, I stare at the structure. Eleazor, as old as my father, was an established merchant of some wealth, while I was merely a young girl with no status. Yet there existed between us an equality. We spoke of many things, we laughed, we thought. Eleazor became to me all that I was not. To him I gave completion. How grateful to the Lord God we were for our blessings.

Two little boys, in pursuit of a cat, race by and abruptly my review ends. Shadows have all but disappeared. I hurry back to the marketplace.

"Figs! Sweet figs! Girl, buy these sweet figs!"

I recognize the voice and the soiled seller.

"Abigail," I cheer, "how good it is to see you!"

We embrace and I feel my morning wash is lost.

"How are you, child?" presses Abigail. "I've not seen you for a long while. Fat Nabod tells me you married his boy."

"I am fine," I respond, surprised at how unfine I feel.

"Tell me about your husband. Is he like his father?"

"Not in appearance, but his manner is like Nabod's . . . proper and polite."

Abigail covers her mouth with a grimy hand. "Proper and polite." She giggles, then adds, "That's Nabod, all right, proper and polite."

Her smiling ends as her eyes search out my essence. I realize that I am about to expose my soul.

"Is your husband kind, Marah?"

"He is not unkind."

Her dirty hands squeeze mine and I feel touched by love.

"Oh, Abigail, Heber is so involved with his goats. I wish even once he would speak of something besides the herds. I try to be interested, I even hold the newborn kids. I help with the wounded, I . . . I, oh, I am afraid I will go mad!"

"Marah," soothes this strange woman, "my little friend."

She offers no advice, no counsel, but I sense that I am understood. Knowing that, I feel new strength to cope with Heber's lacks.

Abigail smiles and hands me a fig. I move away. Her call follows, "Figs, fresh figs. . . ."

It is past sunset when we arrive home. Heber does not greet us, he is yet with the flocks.

Goats, I reluctantly conclude, are intelligent creatures. They also have an inclination to mischief. They tease me by nibbling on my clothes, threatening my lunch, or charging me. I am constantly on guard against a lowered head. These creatures mean to butt.

The bucks, especially, delight in this battle game. Somehow they manage to withstand tremendous clobberings. These goats not only challenge each other, but enthusiastically bash trees, rocks, or any target capturing their attention.

The rain comes with suddenness. The ground cannot soak up the deluge. Giant puddles of thick mud abound. Today I am home helping Anna with the endless piles of mending. Earlier this morning Nabod left to aid Heber with the flocks. Anna and I see him now returning. Poor Nabod—he is soaked, his garments wet and heavy. His few sparse hairs gather into dripping strands. This lubberly man will come into the house miserable and shivering, but he will be proper and polite. Yes, Abigail is right. No matter what, Nabod will be proper and polite.

However, as Nabod puffs toward the comfort and shelter of home, a sandal sticks in the deep mud. He bends to retrieve the vanishing shoe, unaware of what a tempting target he has become for an alert, nearly-200-pound he-goat. The great buck lowers his head and charges.

Anna and I yell a warning, but too late. Nabod

flies as a round, robed bird. And oh, the landing! A sprawled, sputtering, muddied Nabod is not proper.

This evening, I observe, he is not even polite.

FIVE

"Is there any way to stop the he-goats from being so smelly?"

The gathered family suspends breakfast eating to gawk at me. The children shriek with a glee made of superiority. Seeking to defend my comment, I suggest, "Perhaps we could bathe them."

Again, great rolls of laughter. "We could put some of your perfume on the bucks," offers one of the boys. The uproar of amusement is deafening, but over the guffaws I hear another brother say, "Maybe we could feed the goats only flowers!"

I rise and glare at the lot of them. They think they are so funny. I am upset and getting shaky.

"Perhaps a goat must stink, but I cannot understand why you have to pick up the odor on yourselves!" I focus on the silent Heber. "It all makes me sick!"

With that I march out of the house, walk a short distance, and throw up.

It is several days later when Anna confronts me.

"Marah, you have been ill for several mornings now."

"I know. Probably I should not be eating so much sour cheese. But lately it is so tasty to me."

Anna sucks in a mouthful of air, releasing it in a low, swishing whistle. "My daughter, I think there is a simple explanation to this. I believe you may be with child."

Now it is my turn to gasp. "With child? Me?"

Anna beams. "It happens."

A few weeks later it is a certainty.

I race to the slope where Heber is caring for an injured doe.

"Heber!"

Startled, he drops the ointment and the goat. "What is it? What is wrong?"

Before he can venture a guess I pull his hand and place it upon my abdomen. "Be very still."

Puzzlement fills Heber's face, but he makes not a sound.

"There! Did you feel it? That was our baby moving. Heber, we are going to have a baby!"

He sinks to the grass, his eyes never leaving mine. Then the unbelievable happens. Heber rolls on the ground, he laughs, and he hollers. Stunned, I watch as he pounds the turf and joyously yells his pleasure. Is it possible that anything unrelated to goats can so delight him?

"A son, Marah, a son!" He punches the air with

his staff. "We are going to have a son to join me in the herding of my flocks!"

Grinning, he collapses. I look down at his ecstatic face. "Our baby might be a girl," I caution, "or if a son, he may choose to be other than a goatherd."

Heber shakes his head and patiently explains, "No, my wife, within you grows my son." He leaps to his feet and stretches out his arms, indicating the scope of the herds. "His life will be as my own . . . spent here among the goats."

"Marah! Wake up!"

I push off the rough hands as part of a bad dream.

"MARAH!" Her voice urges me into wakefulness.

"What is wrong?" I ask, now fully alert.

"Thieves, that is what. We were awakened by the dogs and then one of the hired men burst in, announcing that the goats near the house were in danger. The men and boys are already out there. We must join them lest even more be lost!"

I shuffle my feet into sandals and grab a long stick used in tending the nearby animals. Thus armed, I join Anna and strike out into the night.

The flock is in panic. Their frightened bleatings, the frenzy of the dogs, the shouts from the men, mingle into one confused horror.

Ahead, in the dim light of the crescent moon, a shadowy figure moves. Stealthily I approach the stranger. Under his arms two small goats wriggle. Clutching the pole in both hands, I tighten my grip as concern for Heber's flock fills me with an unknown bravado. Lunging at the culprit, I whack him across the back. Before he can respond I add a quick blow to the side of his head. Caught by surprise and pain, the screaming thief hurls the kids to the dirt. He charges with clenched fists, striking first my shoulder, then my jaw.

Being somewhat frail these days, and now frightened, I crumble. Anna sees the occurrence. She is neither frail nor frightened. Two sizable stones propelled by rage and a torrent of orders dissuade the scoundrel from anything save flight.

The first light of day reveals the losses. Several of the younger goats are missing. Two does, severely gashed during the fray, have to be destroyed. I almost wish the thieves had taken every goat. Then, perhaps, my husband might focus a little on me.

My face is swollen and discolored. Sharp pains run from my shoulder to my back and left arm. However, the wound which pains me most is Heber's lack of caring. Oh, he is sorry I am hurt. He even applauds my stand against the intruders, but his deepest regard, as usual, is for the goats.

Anna cares, however. Dear, sweet Anna. She squeezes out the faded cloth and gently bathes my injured jaw. I am moved by the tenderness on her round face. Without warning my tears gush forth. For these bruises I begin to cry. Once started, I mourn for my beautiful Sebaste, my parents, and Eleazor. I sorrow, remembering the harshness of the Roman soldiers toward a countryman. I lament over Heber's callousness. And finally I weep for my unborn baby, destined to live with goats.

Anna too, shares in the emotional cleansing and wails for her own years of hardship.

This done, we prepare breakfast.

My feet are no longer visible to me. The thin rope Anna provides for a measure affirms that my middle is greatly expanding. Assured that my unborn child is steadily growing, I wrap the rope into a loose circle and place it under the outside bench. My baby is active for longer periods of time. I complain that a herd gone berserk stampedes within me.

"Don't fret," chuckles Anna, "babies must stretch and move about. All mine did. And look how healthy and bright they are."

Without question, Nabod and Anna have produced a healthy family. But bright? Long ago Nabod's education ended due to the early death of his father. He is not foolish, just simple in his concerns. Daily I hear the family's chatter and opinions, but their talk is shallow, limited.

I suspect that Anna has had deep experiences. Perhaps the day will come when we will talk deeply.

Nabod's chief drive is the gaining of wealth. Over the years he has struggled, not for wisdom, but for that opportunity which would make him a rich man. At last, as merchant of Heber's goats, Nabod has found that occasion for prosperity.

I recall his glee over my large dowry. With the inheritance of my parents, plus that of Eleazor's, I held considerable wealth. Following my marriage to Heber I have watched as Persian rugs, ivory tables, and damask couches, once mine, changed into goats. Furnishings not sold add to the already abundant clutter of this house. Anna holds the purse fat with coins.

I have endured the loss of my possessions without much distress. But one privation I continue to nurse and grieve. We do not attend Sabbath services.

"Someday, daughter," Nabod assures, "we will go to the *kinshaw*. But for now, we are content to steadfastly honor the day's restrictions. Be at peace."

An overcast sky ushers in this Sabbath morning. The entire household is quiet, observing holy rest. Inasmuch as fires are forbidden, we sit in a darkened house. No cooking is possible, no warmth to counter the day's chill. Yet within me, a hidden baby stirs and kindles an unseen flame, filling me with warmth and brightness. Since Eleazor's death I've not genuinely extolled the goodness of the Lord God. But now this new life moves within my swelling body. *God be praised,* I silently sing, in spite of no worshiping congregation to join in my adoration.

The stars are competing in brilliance against the deep blue Samaritan night sky. Sounds are only the familiar ones, bringing a mood of repose to the sleeping family. I lie wide awake, suddenly

unconcerned with stars and sounds . . . for a
strong inner rolling sensation holds my notice. I
sit up and wait. Soon these sensations grow into
obvious contractions. The proper response
seems clear. I shout my news, "It is happening!
The baby is coming!"

In an instant the house springs into an uproar.
The smaller children whimper at being awakened, while the older ones race to my side to
watch. Heber shivers and stares. Nabod, true to
form, gives polite orders to Anna, who for weeks
has had all things in readiness. Her assured manner soothes everyone. A quick smacking of her
hands magically clears my bedroom of observers.

Lifting me to my feet, Anna directs me to be
seated on the nearby ebony bench. Once this
had stood by my mother's dressing table. It comforts me to rest upon it now.

My round kinswoman is at home in her current role of midwife. Anna spreads a clean linen
cloth over the several mattresses she has piled.
"Rest here," she instructs, pointing to the newly
made bed.

I gratefully watch the preparations. First a
table is brought close to my bed. On this Anna
places the largest lamp. Beside it she sets a
pitcher of water.

Anna grins as she carries in the small basket to
cradle the infant. It is filled with strips of cloth.
"Bands for the child," she explains.

"Anna, I have seen goats give birth." I take her
hand. "Will it be the same for me?"

"People are not goats." She laughs, patting
my face.

I watch the pale light of dawn silhouetting the low hills outside my narrow window. The stars linger as though reluctant to miss the event. Still I struggle and wonder at the long delay. Anna murmurs encouragement that all is going well. I am not convinced.

I did not know it would be so long, I think, or this difficult. For goats it seems much easier. Yet all they ever get is goats.

The sun is climbing upward when at last I smile a glad welcome to my firstborn. Anna's experienced hands knowingly rub my red little son with the salted water. Then, smoothing his new skin with oil, she coos, "What a fat fine boy you are."

Wrapped in my own bands of joy and exhaustion, I watch Anna swaddle the wiggling baby. Preparation for the presentation to Heber is completed.

I lie back on my bed, close my eyes, ready to submit to the alluring call of sleep, but first. . . .

"His name is Aaron," I settle. Somehow it seems too presumptuous to call him Moses.

SIX

Of course it has happened before. Babies are born everyday, I know this. And yet . . .

I hold Aaron and perceive something utterly new, pristine, and uniquely mine. At once I am singular in privilege while bonded with all womankind. What mystery has formed and shaped within me another being? Is it God who called forth this child? I touch Aaron's wee chin. How can I explain the perfections of this infant face?

Awed, thrilled, and overwhelmed, I rock my baby and sing.

Firstborn,
tiny, soft.
What funny small noises you make.
Your feet are
topped with toes
no bigger than

spring's buds.
Miniature hands
curled into tight fists.
Let me peek into them.
Perchance
they hold stars.
This day my heart is immersed in joy,
for Aaron is my sweet baby boy.

I meander about the house, momentarily free of inhabitants, and share information with my dark-haired son. "This, Aaron, this largest room is the gathering room. See the low, wide table circled with cushions? The family assembles here for meals. Over there in that corner, where so many mattresses are piled, Grandpa Nabod and Grandma Anna sleep."

Someday I will tell him of his other grandparents, but for now I show him the ivory table that once was theirs. "Here." I place his little hand upon the table's top that he might feel the smoothness. "Isn't that nice?"

We weave through the route of the house, examining every item and feature. In addition to the main room, an annex stands on either side. The larger is divided in two, and serves as bedroom for the many children. The lesser room, once used for storage, now houses Heber, Aaron, and me.

"You were born here, my son, right in this room, only four months ago. And in this same room I hope to give birth to many sons and daughters." I recall the times I longed for a sibling. Aaron must not know such loneliness.

43

My baby seriously attends to my words and responds with a thoughtful outpouring of spit bubbles.

I playfully tickle his tummy while he chortles his merriment. "Someday, Aaron, you will know everything I know, and more. You will be aware of life beyond goats."

This morning Heber collected all his brothers and sisters to assist him in the numbering of goats. Until Aaron is older I am free of herd responsibilities. Anna is happy to have my assistance in her countless tasks.

Aaron drifts off to sleep while nursing. Careful not to awaken him, I place him on his side in his hamper to nap. Moments ago, Anna, balancing a great stack of baskets, waddled out to the fig orchard. Now free, I join her.

"Could you use some help?"

Anna wipes the moisture from her forehead with the back of her hand. Her cheeks, bright red, look like fresh pomegranates. "Yes I do. These figs ripen faster than I can collect them. And I just am not able to climb to the high branches. Here, take this basket and see if you can do anything about those uppermost figs."

Being agile, I find it no problem to scale the sprawling trees. Broad leaves spread an awning about me and I work in shade. The tree yields the dark fruit as though happy to be rid of the burden.

"Anna, have you ever noticed that the ripe fig is both purple and brown?"

My mother-in-law drops her arms to her portly

sides, "Oh my, child, you notice things I do not even see." She laughs as she pushes the wayward hair off her forehead. "My thoughts were all caught up with how to get these figs into my children without hearing their complaint, 'All we ever get to eat is figs!'"

And so we pluck the purple-brown harvest, planning menus featuring camouflaged figs. Pleasantly the time passes as we share work and prattle, even occasionally speaking of important matters.

Abruptly Anna sets aside a half-filled basket. "Come out of that tree and join me for a little rest in the shade."

I find that a most suitable idea.

Finished at last with her long drink of water, Anna offers me the earthen jar. The cool liquid satisfies. I lean my head against the tree and close my eyes.

Anna gently seizes my chin between her thumb and forefinger and turns my face-toward her questioning eyes. "The goats bother you, don't they dear?"

Taken aback, I feign a cough. "It isn't the goats," I say, smoothing the wrinkles from my skirt.

"What is it then that grieves you so?"

Anna's eyes are kind. She is not prying, she knows I bear a hurt and seeks only to bring healing. Perhaps this is the time for our substantial conversation.

"It isn't the goats, it really is not the goats." I had meant my secret to be well hidden, but now here is Anna peering into my private store of thoughts. Words tumble out before I can check them.

"Oh, Anna, it is Heber's total love for the herds! How can I matter to him when he only has eyes for the goats?"

She offers a mediating word. "A man must give time and care to his livelihood."

"I know that. I try to understand his interest, and I do admire his skill. But I am weary of every thought, every word, every concern centering on goats!"

Anna nods her head for me to continue.

"If I mention our baby, the overhead sun, Rome's rule, the flower gardens of Samaria, or the weather, Heber relates the subject to goats. Sometimes it baffles my mind how he does it, but he does. Once I plainly announced that I did not want to talk about anything to do with the flocks."

"And?"

"All day he considered me witless and told me not to bother him with foolish words about other things."

"Do you not have times of just laughing together and chatting of nothing?"

"No."

"Can my son only speak of goats to a woman?"

"Just goats."

The plump, agitated woman shakes her head and rubs the back of her short neck. "Daughter, he desires you as a man desires his wife . . . surely he does not mention the herds then?"

"When Heber's voice is low with tenderness,

when his words hold passion, it touches goats. Even dear Aaron is not loved as a son. His father cares for him as a potential goatherd." I pause to swallow the growing fullness in my throat. Tears begin and I decide to let them flow.

"What am I to do? I honored duty and married my kinsman. I try, Anna, I try so hard. Please help me to understand Heber. Perhaps, then, I can deal with my ferment."

With a fig-stained finger Anna clears my cheeks of the remaining tears. Deliberately she makes herself comfortable. I suspect her answer will not be brief.

"Several years ago Nabod fixed a large broken wall for a man. In payment the man gave Nabod a few young goats. At first we saw them as merely pets. In fact, Marah, long ago you visited and played the whole afternoon with the goats. Well, before long we noticed that these animals needed more care than we felt we could give. Goat-tending didn't suit Nabod, and I was busy with babies. Somebody had to see that the creatures were cared for, so the responsibility fell on Heber. For a boy of eleven he did a fine job.

"One evening as Nabod and I discussed the soon coming into manhood of our oldest son, we wondered what present to give him. At length we decided to make the boy owner of every single goat. Heber was elated. He studied the creatures, and what he couldn't figure out on his own he asked at the marketplace. Soon he knew everything anybody could know about herding. After only three years, the flock had grown so large that Nabod became his son's merchant.

Unlike other herders, who leave the work to hirelings, Heber tends his own animals. The goats are a fine livelihood for all of us."

"I still do not understand why they should capture my husband's mind, heart, and soul!"

Anna's graying eyebrows lift as a flash of insight alights her face. "I think I know, I think I just might know." I lean forward so as not to miss a word. "Somehow, my daughter, the goats point to Heber's manhood. Success with the flocks makes him important . . . gives him a sureness. I do believe that is why the creatures mean so much to him. Can you understand that?"

"In a way. But I still wish Heber could see beyond the goats to his wife and son and. . . ."

Aaron's cries end our confidences.

"Thank you, Anna, for telling me this. Thank you for caring that I know." I kiss her quickly, pick up the baskets of figs, and dash to my demanding baby.

Aaron's complaining ceases immediately when he spies me. He smiles, squeals, and flaps his fat arms and legs in greeting. I marvel anew at the wonder of this fair child. He grasps my forefingers and of a sudden I recognize that he holds more than a bit of my flesh. Those small, dimpled hands embrace the whole of my devotion, the entire of my being.

Could this be how it is with Heber and his goats? Does he find his worth with the herd even as I do with Aaron? I pick up my gurgling son and press our cheeks together. This baby is my life. Heber has found his with his goats. I purpose to be more understanding of my husband's enthrallment with his animals.

"He is big enough." Heber is adamant. "The boy will not learn a thing about herding merely by staying with the goats that graze near the house. It is time he meets the animals out on the slopes."

Isn't it sufficient that goats own my husband? Must I give up my baby to them as well? I argue, plead, and even bring out a few tears, but to no avail. *Aaron, not yet three, is to be goatherd.*

To my dismay, our son is delighted with everything relating to goats. Heber proudly teaches the child. "Goats are intelligent animals," he begins. Although I've joined the work to be near Aaron, I shudder and move away to rid myself of the oft-heard words.

However, Aaron is in paradise. Every day, following his father's lessons, the boy dashes to play. He climbs the rocks, chases the young goats, and romps with the dogs. Tanned, sturdy, and jubilant, Aaron savors all the glory of being a child. These days pass without hurry. I consider my husband, my son, and the goats, and resign myself to accept life as it is.

The afternoon is hot. Heber and I succumb to dullness. My shepherd husband frets that I might accidentally injure a goat with my overly heavy staff and begins the carving of a new rod. From the brief shade of a young tree, I half watch Heber at work whittling and half watch Aaron who is never still. Seeing our lethargy, the child knows he must make his own fun. From the pile of old rags used for tending wounds of the goats, Aaron finds a long strip of tattered linen. He swishes the scrap through the still air. The field is his. Aaron stomps about, waving aloft his newly found banner, hollering little boy words of exuberance.

Suddenly I am caught in a sickening terror. I see a large buck, accepting the flag's challenge, about to charge. Frantic, I shout an alarm. Aaron stops his play and questioningly looks at me. Then he spies the racing brute. Stunned by fear, the youngster stands wide-eyed and motionless.

Aaron! O God, help me rescue my son!

Screaming, I swing my weighty staff; I tear to Aaron's defense. Before I can span the distance, the huge goat butts Aaron with a brutal savagery. As I reach the beast I submit eagerly to an insane frenzy of revenge and slam my rod upon the goat's back. The buck, bleating his protest, runs away. My fury shall not be thwarted. I give chase. Coming upon the animal, I thrash the dark fur with my club again and again and again.

Heber, now at the scene, forces my arms down. "Enough, woman, enough! Can't you see the animal is dead?" My weapon falls.

With profound dread I approach the small crumpled body thrown to the outcropping of stones. Gently I lift the curl-topped head. Aaron's blood, warm upon my hand, causes my heart to chill. These hideous wounds will not pain my once-laughing son.

Heber stares at Aaron, the goat, and me. Slowly he backs away and spreads his tunic on the ground. Heber lifts the carcass of the buck onto the garment, wraps it, and with downcast eyes leaves.

I gather the lifeless form of Aaron. Leaning against a great boulder, I tenderly cradle my boy. "Please, Aaron," I kiss the closed eyes, "oh, please, please!" For a long while I rock him and sob my anguish. Finally I rise and stumble toward the house.

Rage grows in the soil of grief. My heart pounds with torment. Confronting heaven, I roar, "Lord God! You! Do you hear me? When my parents died I yet believed in your goodness. Even when death claimed Eleazor I did not question you. But this! This is too much! How could you allow a cursed goat to kill by baby? Look at him!" I lift my bloodied son skyward, that God might better view him. Sobbing, choking, I reel forward, overcome by agony. "Does it please you to permit this? Does it? Oh, how can you even know what I am suffering?

"Will you ever have to know what it is to watch a beloved son cruelly die?"

SEVEN

Aaron is gone. My dear little boy is no more.

I scan the trees for a robust climber. *Empty.* Upon earth's grasses I look for a laughing tumbler. *Empty.* I peer into my arms for a nestling, sleepy child. *Empty.*

My world is void. Laughter, love, and life all fled before the battering of a goat.

Today is chilly. The cold wind forces the family indoors. The din and activity are considerable. I find it impossible even to breathe in here. I slip my cloak about my shoulders and wander a short distance from the house.

For a long while, I watch the churning of dark clouds. The wind moans and pushes against me, whipping my clothes and disheveling my hair. Heavy gusts cause the brushwood to writhe. The rains surely will soon begin.

I startle at the unexpected weight of a hand upon my arm. It is Anna.

"The wind blows hard today."

I nod, not caring to speak.

"Marah, dear, we've all grieved for Aaron these past three months."

I turn and our eyes meet. Tenderness passes between us.

"You will have more sons," she whispers.

I yield to Anna's leading and return to the clatter of the family.

Through the tasks of following days I move, guided only by habit. The mornings dawn, but night covers me. The bird lifts her voice, yet I hear no song. People surround me and I am alone.

Aaron is gone. My dear little boy is no more.

"Marah," states Heber, "your help is needed on the slopes. Soon the does will be dropping their young. Plan on joining me early next week."

Without further comment, he walks out the door. What was that all about? Since Aaron's death he seemed to accept my refusal to herd. Why is he now insisting? But insist he does. Every time we are together he tells me that I am to tend goats.

Anna and I finish cleaning up things following the evening meal. Heber pulls me to the cushion near his.

"Tomorrow you will join me on the slopes. I want to explain to you which does need watching and what injuries you should check."

Puzzled by his persistence, I again explain,

"Heber, I've told you many times that I can never return to the herds."

He laughs and shakes me slightly. "Of course you can. I think you are using grief as an excuse not to work."

Perhaps he is right. I do hate herding. But surely Heber realizes my compelling reason for avoiding the flocks. I look into his harsh face and force a smile . . . and once more flatly refuse.

My husband's tanned hands grip my wrists. His voice equals the scowl of his face. "I thought with time you'd leave your sadness. Now, Marah, I plainly tell you, shake off the grief! I've been patient long enough."

This growing contest strengthens my resolve. "I'm sorry, but I cannot go with you."

Heber's eyes widen and fasten upon mine. "You are my wife." Tightening his hold, he demands, "And you will join me, you will come!"

I jerk away from him. "NO! Every bleating, every butting . . . no, I will not return to the herds, *ever!*"

These words of rebellion startle me. Not only have I raged against heaven, now I defy my husband.

Heber jumps to his feet and stomps toward the door. He starts to speak, pauses, then blurts loudly, "You killed my buck! The very one that sired many of my best goats. What good did it do to lose your head and destroy the animal?"

The family is absolutely still. Not one word of this confrontation dare be missed. I hold no wish to disappoint their impolite curiosity. For the first

54

time since Aaron's death I know an emotion other than grief.

"You fault me for killing the creature that bashed our son to death? How can you possibly scold me? Which life mattered most to you, husband, the goat or the boy?"

Heber jerks at the door, the strong door only recently placed to keep out the house goats. "You judge me unfairly." In a tone barely audible, he hisses, "You should not have wasted the life of my goat!" With that he slams the door behind him.

In the days following our dispute, I attempt words of peace, hoping to relieve our war. I am milking the house goats when Heber comes in from the fields.

"I'm surprised to see you lower yourself and touch a goat." The sarcasm of his words stings.

"Please, Heber, let's try to talk without bitterness."

He considers me with distaste. "You are a disappointment to me." His voice is controlled and condemning. "I had hoped you'd be a full wife."

I stop milking. How can he say that? Never have I slighted any known need of his. My only lack is with the goats. In that sense he says the truth.

I start to speak, venturing to resolve our difficulties.

"Oh shut up, woman. I am sick to death of the sight of you."

Days pass, and every meeting with my husband ends in bitter quarreling. Nabod and the children ally with Heber and shun me. Only Anna continues to be my friend.

It is late into the night. Heber is with his goats. In the far corner Nabod loudly snores. The children have been asleep for hours. During this long evening Anna and I have lingered at the table watching the burning of the lamp's low flame soften the darkness. Between us is an awkward, atypical silence. Anna breaks a piece of bread in two and speaks.

"I'm sorry things are so bad."

Trying to word my thoughts, I run my finger unhurriedly around the cup's edge. "Anna, it is all hopeless. The memory of that day haunts me. Did you know that Heber never even touched Aaron, but only the goat? He placed the beast onto his own cloak and carried it away in his arms."

Anna, mother of Heber, offers defense. "The goat's blood would have attracted wild creatures. He had to move it."

"And Aaron's blood? Wouldn't it also be sweet to wild animals? No, Anna, it was the buck he tenderly wrapped and held. Little Aaron was left to me. My husband walked away from us. I can't push that from my memory."

Anna shakes her head.

I continue, "Heber's world destroyed mine. There is no way I can work to build his. Reconciliation is impossible."

Anna pushes aside the hairs cascading over her forehead. "What are you going to do?"

This question, obsessing me for weeks, surprisingly finds an immediate answer.

"I am leaving." *There, it is said.*

Anna smacks her round cheeks. I jump at the sound. Nabod does not even stir.

"Leaving?"

"Anna, I've tried to bring peace. I've tried many times, and failed."

My mother-in-law clutches my hands to her short neck. "I want you here with me." Slowly she raises my fingers to her lips. Then, dropping my hands, she sighs, "Not all marriages are pleasant. Quarrels, misunderstandings, and troubles are part of living. You were overly pampered by your parents and later protected from any hardship by Eleazor. But now, now you are a woman, wife of a goatherd. You must live with people, with things as they are. I wish my son were, well, I wish he were different. But Heber is what he is. Can't you just accept that?"

"Every encounter with Heber leads to bickering and concludes with his demand that I get out of his sight."

"But, Marah! That doesn't mean that you should leave!" Laying her head onto her arms, Anna weeps uncontrollably. I stroke her hair until her sobbing eases. "Anna, please listen to me."

She wipes her wet face with the back of her hand. "Forgive me. I can listen now."

"It is more than my frustrations and sorrows that drive me away. I am concerned about other children I may bear. What is to be their fate? Am I to produce more targets for the whims of goats?

"And look at the division I bring to your family. Neither Nabod nor the children even speak to me. Soon, if I stay, that hostility will be directed at you. I can't stand to be the cause of a rift between you and your family. I must leave. My love for you urges me to go."

It is very late. Wispy shadows, drawn by the flickering lamp, cavort upon the walls. Nabod's snoring has ended for the time being. Reluctantly my mother-in-law nods her acceptance of my decision.

"Will you go back to Sebaste?"

It really doesn't matter where I go. Life means little to me. I start to say this, but am hushed by the anxiety in Anna's dark eyes. She needs to picture me living comfortably someplace. I manage a smile and say, "I've always wanted to look upon the Great Sea. Caesarea is a thriving city. A woman, skilled with a needle, should be able to find work there."

Anna returns my smile. "That is so. You do know how to mend." For several minutes she reminisces over the mounds of garments I helped her repair. Then she abruptly stops speaking, spits on her fingers, and pushes the straying hairs in place. "But dear, it is not safe for a woman to travel alone. Rome insists the highways are safe for all. But we know better. An unprotected woman faces certain danger."

Her words are too true. It is foolish for a woman to travel alone on the highway. If only I were a man. "Anna! That's it! I'll travel as a young man."

Anna scowls. "God does not allow women to be men."

I am not comfortable with God-talk. However,

I answer Anna. "I am not suggesting that I pose as a man for any reason save my safety. I can't believe that counters God's purposes."

Anna rubs her chin and chuckles. "With your green eyes and brown, silky hair? Nay, you are too pretty to be anything other than a woman." She pulls me to my feet and paces around me. "Still . . . yes! We can do it. You are slender, daughter, but not that slender. We'll need to bind your body. With your hair brushed back and secured, and boy's clothing and a staff, you could be a young shepherd on an errand." Excited by her plan, she cackles a bit too loudly. Nabod jerks and snorts, then resumes his noisy slumber.

Whispering, Anna continues, "Marah, I'll miss you more than I can ever tell you."

I try to express my heart, but fail. "Wait here," I tell her. On tiptoe I hurry to my room and return with my childhood prize.

"This is my magical box," I say, placing it before her. Anna listens to its story. "Dear Anna, I want you to keep this box. Remember me whenever you look upon it and know for all time that I love you."

Anna beams as she strokes the smooth ivory. Then her practical nature takes charge. "We must decide the time of your leaving. I suggest it be long before dawn. "What do you think?" And so we plot my future flight. Night after next, when everyone is soundly sleeping, I will go from this house.

Alone in my room, I reflect upon that lovely box. I yet see Anna's plump red hands touching the creamy white of the ivory and the bulging glass. In the slight shining of the lamp those small pieces of glass were empty of color. How like my life . . . all the color and brightness have vanished.

Aaron is gone. My dear little boy is no more.

EIGHT

Hidden beneath my mattresses lies the packed satchel. Stuffed with tightly rolled clothing and womanly grooming needs, it awaits travel.

This very night my planned exodus will happen. Guilt plagues me. Wives do not walk out on husbands. I entered this marriage to honor duty. Now I flee that very service. My trespass tugs at me, yet I recognize its bindings are fraying threads.

Again, following supper, Anna and I remain at the table. Heber hasn't been home for several days. I am glad he isn't here tonight. Nabod and the children sleep. In low tones, we women chat, reviewing the past, sometimes laughing, sometimes crying.

Nabod's house lies less than five miles northwest of Sebaste. A major highway runs between Sebaste and Caesarea. We chart the best way for me to reach that road. My entire journey will be mostly through hilly country.

Anna bounces about the room securing boy's clothing. She spreads the gathered items across the table. Smoothing the rough, dark fabric, Anna decides, "Brown is a good color for a shepherd." The job of changing my appearance begins with the binding of my torso. My long hair is brushed back, knotted, and secured. Anna the resourceful brings forth a bowl containing a mixture of dirt and ashes. "Shepherds—especially the young ones—do not stay clean for long." We lightly rub the soil over my skin and costume. As my mother-in-law fastens the headpiece, she pronounces my transformation complete.

"Dear, you must remember to walk with boyish step. Sling the satchel over your shoulder and use the staff to measure out long strides." She demonstrates and we both are caught by laughter that must be kept silent.

Earlier in the day, at Anna's insistence, I had rested. Now, feeling alert and strong, I am eager to be on my way. Anna tucks a gorged purse into my already full satchel. "It may be some time before you earn money. Besides, it seems reasonable that you should have some of the dowry back." From a shelf she hands me a package. "Lunch," she explains. Amused, I remember that any meal not shared around the table is "lunch."

Cautiously we open the door and step into the night and the parting. For an instant I don't think I can bear leaving her.

"Anna," I cry, wrapping my arms about her.

She hugs me to her ample self and I lose my balance. "Thank you, dearest Anna, for all you are to me. May all your days be glad."

She wipes the forming tears from her eyes and advises, "Marah, think only upon the times that were pleasant. Do not hold on to bitterness." Her fingers caress my moist cheek. "Dear daughter, I shall miss you."

I hold the hand blessing me and fill it with kisses.

"God go with you, Marah."

We embrace for the last time and then she disappears into the house. I stare at the shut door, hesitating. A few of the house goats bleat at me. With a wave I answer, "Good-bye, goats." In lower voice I add, "Good-bye, Heber."

Right off, I try the long steps of boyish walk. This style is unnatural for me. And uncomfortable. Male bones must be constructed differently. Or else how are men able to move this way in ease?

It is not the balance of walking, however, that disquiets my mind. On the edge of desired exile, I waver between despair and hope. On this thin border, I tremble between what was and what might be.

Anna's face, so filled with caring, comes to mind. By this time she is snuggled into her mounds of mattresses and joins Nabod in snores. Her farewell words repeat themselves, "God go with you."

After all my ragings, will he indeed go with me? Even as I run away from my husband, will he follow?

"God go with you," Anna had said. Strangely, these words comfort.

At last I find the highway. A large rock rises by the edge of the road, one side holding a trace of heat from yesterday's sun. I rest by it and warm my back. It is pleasant to relax and not have to think.

My hand brushes against the food package. I decide to snack. Dear Anna has sent a banquet of cheeses, figs, spice cakes, and shelled almonds. It is all so palatable that I eat more than I intended. Opening my water flask, I sip a few swallows.

Refreshed, I stand, stretch, and look up. The star-pocked sky reaches to forever. Dawn comes soon. For only a little longer darkness reigns. The highway is deserted. I am the lone traveler. Freed of audience and responsibilities I run, jump, and kick pebbles just as I did long ago.

Subtly color returns, contouring the land. The easterly horizon spills gold and lavender into the world before me. I admit that some of the murkiness of my despair has gone with the night.

A sudden thunder of running horses breaks dawn's hush. Rome's armies race toward me. I leap off the road. My heart's beating matches the rhythm of the pounding hooves. Has Heber sent them? They come from the direction of Sebaste. Stone-still, I watch their hurried passing. Certainly those determined riders pursue more than a culpable wife. Nevertheless, I stay far off the road until they vanish. Catching my breath and locating my belongings, I resume travel.

"Lad! You there, lad!"

I look around and realize I am the "lad."

Sitting spread-eagled, just off the road, is an old man. A gray old man—his hair, scraggly beard, face, and tunic all are gray. If voices came in color, I am sure his would be gray.

"Come here, young man! I need help. Did you see those soldiers tearing by on horseback?"

"Yes, sir, I did."

"Well, one of those cursed horses kicked up a stone that hit my leg. Now I can't even rise. Don't stand there gawking, boy, get me up!"

I tug and push while he hollers his misery. I'm afraid his leg is broken. He cannot stand.

"No," the old man yells, "it isn't broken, but it hurts!"

His eyes, red and teary, attest to his pain. Gingerly I lift his tunic, revealing a bloodied leg. Frankly I'd like to scream and be on my way. Instead I mutter in proper boy-voice, "Better let me bandage this gash." He agrees. The wrappings of my lunch tear easily. I wind strips about his skinny limb. Poor old man, he is so pale and obviously weak. I ask if he might be hungry.

"Yes, I am," he says and finishes off the last of my food.

"Young man, help me get home. It isn't far, just down the road a stone's throw. Now, give it a try and get me to my feet."

Since I am going that way anyway, I consent. The bleeding has eased and my lunch strengthens him. I prop my staff by his good side and serve as support for the rest of his weight.

"What is your name, lad?"

"Mara . . . uh, Mareshah."

"Mine's Abner."

Half an hour later I inquire just how far he throws stones. He chuckles and says we are almost there and I am not to fret.

It is a considerable way before he points to a cluster of shabby buildings back from the road.

"Go to that one," he orders.

As we approach the designated dwelling, a large figure steps from the doorway. He moves with the grace of a great tree touched by evening wind.

"Abner, what have you done to yourself?" calls the voice, vibrant and masculine. As he nears I almost drop my companion. Before me towers the most handsome man I've ever seen. He wears a short, dusty green tunic, perfect for displaying his bronzed, muscular body. He takes Abner's arm from about my neck and lifts my once-burden as though it weighed not a thing.

Freed, I stand staring. This man's face is exquisite, every feature faultlessly formed and ideally placed. Suddenly he turns and smiles at me. Disgustedly I remember . . . I am a wife, albeit a runaway one. I am yet a wife. Worse, I am a boy.

"Thank you, lad, for helping my friend, Abner," he lightly socks my shoulder.

The gray man explains, "Joel, Rome's soldiers did this. They came tearing down the highway and their no-good horses kicked up a rock that tore into my leg. If this boy hadn't come along and helped me I'd have bled to death, I would."

Joel places Abner on a cot in a littered room of the largest building. He swiftly unbandages

Abner's leg, washes the wound, studies it, and applies an ointment. "I'm sorry, Abner. I shouldn't have left you to walk alone on that road."

"Things would've been worse if you'd been with me. Joel, I never saw riders go that fast!" They laugh uproariously. I fail to understand the joke.

Turning to me the old man points a bony finger. "That lad gave me his lunch. Better find him something to eat. His name is Mareshah." Abner closes his eyes and heaves a sigh. Shaggy gray eyebrows drop, almost covering the closed lids.

Joel spreads a sheepskin over the weary gentleman and motions for me to follow him outside.

"Rest here, son," he points to a narrow bench. "I'll find something for you to eat. By the way, my name is Joel."

I am very tired. Supporting Abner all the way has taxed me. This whole episode delays me. My good food is gone. These bindings are uncomfortable. I really feel a cry is in order, but being a "boy" I do not allow the tears to even begin.

Joel drops onto the bench. "Here, I found some hard bread and wine." His smile unnerves me. I move away, pretending to swat at a gnat.

"Mareshah, where are you heading?"

I remember to talk gruffly. "My parents are dead. I am on my way to Caesarea to find work. Besides, I've always wanted to look at the Great Sea."

"Caesarea does have many jobs for a young man." Joel studies me. "Your eyes are almost the color of the sea itself." I try not to blush.

Joel reties his sandal, then asks, "Do you know anything about herding? I noticed your staff."

Attempting to hide the emotions his question stirs, I cough. Joel slaps my back. "Are you all right?"

"I'm fine, thanks."

"Well, do you know anything about herding?"

"I do."

"Tomorrow Abner and I were to take his two dozen sheep to a buyer near Caesarea. With this leg injury I know he can't manage the trip. If you would help me, I'd pay you. What do you say, friend?"

I consider his offer. These are sheep, not goats. I think I can handle that. More importantly, I would have protection. "Yes," I tell him, "I will help."

"Good!" He whacks my back. "We will leave before the sun is up. How about giving me a hand pulling burrs out of the sheep? This buyer is fussy about that."

We spend the warm afternoon yanking out whatever might be entangled in sheep's wool. I like sheep even less than goats. Finished with that dismal task, we do Abner's bidding. "Get water, stack wood, sweep up that dead brush. . . ."

Evening comes and we collapse onto the run-down benches in front of the largest building. Abner, tyrant of the day, becomes tender. "Thank you, men. I can't think of how I'd have managed without you." Our host is getting misty-eyed. Even his tears are gray. He turns to me, "You were kind to a stranger. May God be with you, son." Once more I am cheered by this benediction.

"Sleep wherever you like, Mareshah," Abner gestures toward the other shacks.

Joel explains, "The old man allows no one but himself to rest in the main house. Over there is my guest cottage . . . always in readiness for my visits. You are welcome to bed down there, too, if you like."

I gulp and try to think fast. "Thank you, but I will sleep elsewhere. I, uh, I snore very loudly and might disturb you."

"Suit yourself, son," shrugs Joel. "Sleep where you will and snore all you wish."

NINE

"Mareshah! Time to wake up!"

"I already am," I shout back, rubbing the sleep from my eyes.

"Come on, then. Abner has breakfast waiting for us."

I recall last night's supper. No need to rush. I adjust the bindings and straighten my tied-back hair. Since I wish to appear totally boy, I leave off washing.

Abner grins as I approach the outside table. "Good morning, son. I hope you slept well. Joel, here, tells me you can handle sheep."

"I've done some herding."

"Good. But watch that Joel," he snickers. "Don't let him make you do all the work. Eat now, boy, eat up. You've a long walk ahead."

Breakfast lacks Anna's touch. The figs are mushy, the dried meat is a chore to chew, and the bread is stale. However, hunger and courtesy dictate that I eat.

As the sun lifts from the horizon, Joel announces that we, too, must be moving.

"Abner, old friend, I left ointment on your table. Dab on a little of the medicine every day. Give your leg a rest and it will mend nicely. After I've finished business in town I'll be back with your sheep money."

They embrace and slap each other's backs.

Unwashed and low-voiced, with satchel slung over my shoulder, I face another day as Mareshah, the shepherd boy. Lifting my staff in salute, I bid good-bye to gray Abner. Poor old man, except for Joel's visits I'm sure little excitement ever comes into his life.

The bleating sheep bob obediently along the road. I wonder about my fellow traveler, so apt at herding and mending legs. Just who is he?

"Mareshah," Joel calls from behind me, "watch those two strays heading your way." I move quickly to convince the delinquent pair that it is better to stay with the others.

"Do you live around here?" shouts my companion. I drop back for easier conversation. "I've lived in and around Sebaste. But, as I told you, I am going to Caesarea."

Joel grins and I am smitten by his almost-dimples, by his perfect teeth, by everything about him. "I'm sure you enjoyed that fair city perched on the hill." He runs his hand through his mass of black curls. "It's no wonder that Rome honors it with her army's legion."

Of truth it is no honor having Rome invade my

beautiful Sebaste with 6,000 soldiers, their servants, horses, and pack animals, but I must be careful with my words. This man, handsome as he is, just might be a Roman spy. I am able to guard my words, but not my feelings.

"It does increase the population . . . not necessarily the beauty!"

Joel laughs. I am pleased that my words amuse him. Smiling, I watch him jog to the front of the herd.

"Have you ever been to Caesarea, Mareshah?" he calls over his shoulder. "No," I answer, wanting to ask him if he has, and what does he do, and where does he live. Instead, I gruffly repeat, "No."

Finished with his work, he moves again to my side and falls in step with my shorter stride. "Caesarea is quite a city, lad. In all the world it is possibly the most beautiful. . . ."

"Not more beautiful than Sebaste!" I inject.

"Wait until you see Caesarea's white marbled buildings set against the blue sea. Even the flowers come in richer hues."

No city could be lovelier than Sebaste. But there is no point in arguing. I decide not to comment further.

Joel must sense my thoughts, for he quickly explains, "Years ago, you know, Caesarea was only a little village. Then it was called Strato's Tower. Herod the Great brought the present day port city into being. He had an ambitious plan to redo all of Palestine."

He is trying to be kind. I, too, must show some grace.

"Yes, sir, I'm aware of his many projects."

Anxious to please Joel, I ask anything I can think to ask about Caesarea. Joel enjoys being teacher, for he recites fact upon fact about the city.

". . . and since Herod courted Rome's favor he named this stunning new seaport after Augustus himself."

I find it hard to really care very much about Caesarea's history with this handsome Joel so near. I also find it hard to hush the racket of my screaming conscience although I repeatedly announce to myself, "I've left Heber . . . and that's that!"

I study Joel's strong face and think he must be a Jew. Yet he travels in a Samaritan province. Everyone knows Jews avoid any meetings with Samaritans.

"Are you from around here?" I hear myself ask.

"I'm from Jerusalem, son. I am a Jew."

Feeling peeved with my boldness, I lower my eyes and mumble, "I thought you might be."

Joel grasps my shoulder. "Mareshah, look at me. I am different from many of my brother Jews. I'm not cut off from Samaritans."

"Oh?"

"Jew, Samaritan, Greek, all of us are caught in the claw of Rome. That unites us, it must."

For a moment he looks skyward. Then he laughs and asks, "Is there anything else you want to know about Caesarea? Go ahead, boy, and bring on the questions."

I reach back into my early education. "Isn't

there a theater overlooking the sea?"

"My young friend, indeed there is. Perhaps someday I can take you there. All the seats face the water. We'll mount the steps to the top row and gaze out to the world's end.

"There is more, you know. With the amphitheater, hippodrome, and aquaducts, the city abounds with attractions."

Joining his light mood, I laugh. "And, of course, Rome also honors Caesarea and stations a legion there."

"Ho, ho, Rome grants more favor than the mere presence of her armies to Caesarea," boasts Joel in mocking voice. "This city houses the very procurator of Rome."

Cautiously I begin to trust my new friend. Surely he is no spy.

"Joel, in all likelihood those mounted soldiers that Abner and I saw were headed to Caesarea on some official business."

"In all likelihood," he answers, turning away from me, but not before I see the smirk cross his face. Joel and the old man had laughed while discussing these soldiers. What could be the joke they share?

Joel thumps my back. "A boy your age will be fascinated by all there is to do and see in Caesarea. By the way, son, how old are you? Fourteen? Fifteen?"

"Your guess is good," I fib. Here I am, a nineteen-year-old woman, twice married, the mother of a dead child, and this man believes me to be a young boy. I am miffed, yet also relieved that my disguise is so convincing. *Anna, how*

74

tickled you'd be if you knew this.

The morning is half spent when we come upon a broad, slow-moving stream. The sheep rush to drink.

"We'll stop here," announces Joel, "and let the animals refresh their thirst. I usually dip in for a good swim."

To my horror he strips and plunges in. "Join me, Mareshah. You need a wash!"

He splashes handfuls of water at me. I dart out of his way. "I'll watch the sheep, Joel. Go ahead and enjoy your swim."

"The sheep will watch themselves." He laughs at my reluctance. Then in serious tone he advises, "At least soak your feet. You walk as though you are very uncomfortable. Did you hurt yourself lifting Abner?"

I run downstream a fair distance. The green water's coolness adds strong appeal to Joel's words. Loosening my sandals I let my feet dangle in the wetness. I close my eyes and pretend I am yet a little girl and nothing bad has ever happened to me.

"Mareshah, I think I will just pull you in."

Startled from my daydreaming, I see that Joel has floated almost to my feet. He playfully reaches for my ankles. I jump back with the swiftness of a fawn.

"NO! I mean, please, no. You see, sir, I must wait until the Great Sea to bathe. It is a promise I made to myself. Once there, I'll wash off my past and begin a new life." I am amazed at the ease with which I lie.

Joel tilts his head, staring at me. "You are an

odd lad. But very well, my young friend, hold on-to that Samaritan soil until the coast." He swims away and yells from a distance, "By the way, the sea water is salty, very salty."

"I like salt," I mumble.

Fastening my shoes I notice trembling in my fingers. I feel no chill, why then this shaking of my hands? Could it be fear? Or guilt? Or has it anything to do with this handsome Jew?

I look up. Above me stands Joel. He, now dressed, is yet dripping wet. "Mareshah, how long have your parents been dead?"

Truthfully I can answer, "Since I was twelve."

He pulls me to my feet. "Son, life can be hard, but men can be strong." Now he punches my shoulder.

Do men show tenderness to each other only by hitting? I'll be happy to get to Caesarea and once again be a woman.

TEN

Before us rises the great semicircular wall framing the city of Caesarea. Something within quakes and pleads with me to flee. But another something, aggressive and fed by curiosity, urges me forward. Besides, I really have no other place to go.

Selling Abner's sheep took much time. But since then, Joel and I have traveled at a fast pace. The city is all that he promised . . . alive, bustling, and unbelievably beautiful. Flowers in wild colors dazzle my senses.

"Almost as pretty as Sebaste," I tease.

Sunset is at hand when we reach the marketplace. Most merchants remain, eager for the last coins of the day. Joel leads us to the stall responsible for the tempting odors. He presents me a portion of lamb roasted in grape leaves.

Munching the tasty supper, I hurry westward. "Slow down, boy, the sea isn't going to disappear." My companion is right, but all my life I've yearned to look upon this wonder up close.

Overhead white gulls cry as a salt wind carries hints of the shoreline's nearness. We round a corner. Joel leaps ahead, stops, and points.

In front of us lies blue water in unimaginable abundance, the Great Sea itself. Waves, like children in a crowd leaping for a more perfect view, rise, scamper to shore, then stretch upon the land, finally melting back into the ocean. No fence divides, no wall separates, yet an invisible boundary stays the advance of the sea.

I race across the beach and at last kneel at the earth's edge. The water caresses my waiting hand. Numbed by the marvel, I am mindless of time and its passing.

"Now, Mareshah? Now are you going to wash?"

"Soon, Joel." I laugh, boyishly tossing a pebble into the waves.

This handsome man, this kind man, hands me a coin. "For your help with the sheep." Carving the sand with his heel, he adds, "Son, you'll need a place to sleep tonight. I am staying with . . . uh, friends. But I do know of an old shack further down the beach that you may use."

How witless I am. I hadn't even thought of where I might stay. Gratefully I accept Joel's offer.

"You must be out before daybreak. Soldiers patrol the beach and don't take kindly to strangers about."

Our steps slow. I grieve at having to say farewell. Joel's company has been thoroughly pleasant, his words friendly and informative. I'd

78

almost forgotten the satisfaction of companionly conversation. I wish this friendship could continue.

"Behold the fancy inn I told you of." There, tucked under a sand cliff and behind tall grasses, lies the poor shed. "No one will hear you snore in this place," he joshes. "You may stay no more than three nights. Surely in that time you can find housing. And Mareshah, don't make a fire or even light a candle. It is important that you be out by daybreak, returning only after the sun has set." He hits my back. "Thanks for helping old Abner and for herding with me. I hope we meet again."

Watching him amble away, I concur in that hope.

The shed is small and without furnishings. I stand my staff by the doorway and in the waning light unpack a few of my belongings. I am eager to be rid of boy's clothing and soil.

Evening brings a slender moon reflected a thousand times upon the waves. I touch the lapping water with a bared toe. To my pleasure I find the night sea balmy. Not since my arrival has anyone come to this beach. Feeling safely private and very dirty, I slip out of my tunic and bindings and gingerly step into the water. Then deeper. And yet deeper. Only my head remains dry. I untie my long hair and let it bob upon the surface. Surprisingly, I discover that I am buoyant. The waves draw me to shore unless I propel myself otherwise. I dunk my head under and gag. Joel was right. The water is salty. For a long while I play in this new delight. Can it indeed

79

be? Me, all alone in the darkness, splashing in the Great Sea?

Back in my small shelter I find clean woman's clothes. I shake and brush my hair dry. From the alabaster jar I touch the fragrant contents and anoint myself with the perfumed cream. To be clean again is pleasant. To be woman once more is even better.

Over the sandy floor I spread my cloak. It will serve as a mattress, my satchel as a pillow, and the sea as a mother humming lullabyes. My eyelids close and suddenly it is morning.

The marketplace is already a flurry of activity. Hawkers vie for customers. I am hungry for broiled fish, perhaps the nearness of the sea is to blame. The eager merchant before me perceives my mouth is watering and asks a ridiculous price for his wares. I counter. In a flash we are caught in the fire of haggling. After considerable yelling we agree on a price. The fish is delicious. I should have paid more.

Licking my fingers, I amble about the many displays, uncertain as to what it is I seek. Ahead towers a stack of baskets so tall as to hide the seller. Baskets for fruit, baskets for bread, baskets for laundry, baskets for all possessions known to man stand precariously balanced. As I near, two small boys race by, nearly knocking me off my feet. The baskets are not so fortunate. The children crash headlong into the wicker citadel, reducing it to ruin. The frenzied seller is upon the sprawled, frightened villains, threatening doom if repairs are not hastily made. One upturned face catches my attention. A low moan escapes my lips as I remember the small face that once sought mine.

I run away from the scene and weep until tears fail.

A gathering of women catches my notice. They flank a display of fabrics in colors as varied as field flowers. I touch the finery and recall the resolve to find employment as a seamstress. Inquiring as to the whereabouts of the city's favorite dressmaker, I am directed to the shop of Koydal.

Once inside the doorway I find myself face to face with a thin man draped in a long measure of new cloth. More of the same material is spread across the table. Folds of other fabrics lie over the scattered benches. Lint is everywhere.

"I am Koydal," announces the slender owner, bowing low. "How may I serve you, lovely lady? Do you bring your own cloth or do you wish to see some of the fine goods I have right here?"

"Sir, I am looking for a job as a seamstress."

"You do not come to me for a new gown?"

"No sir, I wish work. I need to earn money."

His eyes widen. His expression, only moments ago so humble and intent on pleasing, changes. He steps nearer, tossing the cloth from his shoulders onto the table.

"Do you know how to use a needle skillfully?"

"Yes," I boast.

"Dear lady, do you have references from some other tailor in town?"

"I am new to Caesarea, but I have sewn elsewhere."

"Does your husband work nearby?"

"I am a widow," I answer in half-truth.

Pacing, Koydal scrutinizes me from back to front, from head to toe. I think my sewing abilities are not what interest him. With his long fingers he strokes the back of my hand. "My dear lady, I believe we can find some kind of work for you."

Disgusted by his implication, I jump away and rush back onto the street. Surely there are businesses in this city where my ability to sew is needed.

By noon, after another such encounter, I harbor thoughts about tending goats. Is this entire place composed of lecherous men? By evening I am convinced that it is.

In my shelter once again, I let my thoughts move to Joel. How chaste had been his conversation. Of course he had thought me to be a boy. Still there was no rough talk. I wonder about him. Where does he stay? What is his business in Caesarea? Who are his friends? Will I ever see him again?

I repeat a night dip in the Great Sea. As before, the waters refresh. Yet, discouraged by the day's innuendos, I curl into a corner of the shed. Heber, the goats, and our constant bickering come to mind. Instantly, the shack seems lavish and my predicament almost pleasant. I wrap my cloak about my body and listen to the whispered song of the sea. I have dowry money. Somehow, someway, I will build a secure new life.

A soft scratching outside the back wall startles

me. Motionless, I strain to listen. The scratching repeats, then ends. *Probably a rat,* I conclude, not particularly comforted.

Tomorrow I must find a house.

ELEVEN

Yesterday's experiences with potential employers convince me of the prudence of touring this city as the boy, Mareshah. In this guise I set out for the harbor. Joel whetted my interest to explore the seaport and the special marketplace it breeds.

The sounds of trade, the screaming gulls, and the crashing waves announce the importance of the doings here. It does seem to be the center of world happenings. Numerous merchants march about buying goods to be transported to the inland cities. Exchange is done with an intensity I have never before witnessed. These are merchants dealing with other merchants.

Additional buyers are here, mostly citizens of Caesarea in search of bargains. Some merchandise has been damaged in transit. The ships must be emptied, so the cargo is sold cheaply and with haste.

Instant stalls appear. Sellers, anxious to be rid of newly purchased imports, spread their wares on any available ground. I can't believe the frenzy, the busyness of the whole scene.

I recall Joel's explanation of Herod's dream for a major port surrounded by an imposing city. Since no natural harbor existed here, he hired gifted architects and craftsmen to design and build the breakwater, buildings, massive storehouses, and sailor's quarters.

Herod sought to prove to the world that no error occurred when Rome made this son of Antipater the Idumean, king of the Jews. He brought forth extensive rebuilding programs throughout the land. In Caesarea's port entrance Herod raised gigantic figures of Augustus and Roma. Further, he erected a temple to Caesar, offering ships far out on the sea a visual share in the splendor of Rome.

Reflecting on this, I gaze over the vast stretch of water before me. I am dominated by its scope and presence. In it I see mystery, beauty, and glory, surpassing the best of man's work . . . even that of the great Herod.

Drawn by the scent of baking bread, I push my way through the crowd. The sea air increases my appetite. I buy too much and manage to eat every crumb.

I ought to be looking for a house, but I am fascinated with these surroundings and decide first to browse the shops. Most sellers seem to regard a shepherd as no serious buyer and pay scant notice of me.

I am about to leave the harbor area when a

mound of apparent junk catches my eye. Strewed throughout the mass of disorganized items I spot several boxes similar to my own "magic" box.

Picking up a small box, I inspect the fine detail of the carving. For a moment I regret having given mine away. Then gladness overcomes misgivings as I recall Anna's pleasure with the gift.

From the corner of my eye I see the merchant nearing. "Do you like the box, son? This afternoon I am selling it for much less than it's worth. Almost disgraced am I by such a cheap price!"

I look up. And drop the box on my toe. The seller inspects my face momentarily.

"Marah! Is it really you, child?"

Dirty and wearing an abundance of ragged clothing, she is nevertheless a fair sight.

"Abigail!"

We embrace, laugh, and embrace again.

"Child, what are you doing here? And why are you dressed like that?"

She turns to an elderly man and orders, "Watch the shop for me." He nods and begins the task.

"Come with me," she dictates. "We must talk."

With an expertise I can only attribute to her profession, my guide elbows our way through the swarm of shoppers.

"Where are you staying, Marah? How did you get here?" Her questions increase and I perceive she must read the answers from my face as she gives me no chance to respond.

Abigail leads us a brisk pace out of the market crowd onto a quiet street. Our stride matches. I comment on the new cobblestones set here and there. "The old were broken," she explains.

We turn down a narrow alley. The bordering homes are attractive and well maintained. Passing between larger buildings, we come to a small house. Abigail shushes the barking of a young dog.

"In here," she points.

The room is neat and well furnished. Since I've always pictured this woman sleeping on a pile of dirty rags, I ask whose house this is. Abigail chuckles, "Sit down, Marah, I'll get us some food."

Returning from another room, she plops herself before me and offers fruit from a wide ebony bowl. In this faint interior light, Abigail's filth is not so apparent. I am able to eat.

"How did you recognize me?" I ask. "A man bringing sheep to the outskirts of town hired me to help him. He believed me to be a boy. And besides, it has been four years since we've seen each other. I just can't understand how you knew me so readily."

She runs a hand through her messy hair. "Old Abigail is smart, child. It's hard to fool her. I've known you for all your years. Even though you've grown a span," she titters, "and have turned yourself into a boy, I still know you."

Abigail plies me with numerous questions. To this grubby audience I relate the events of the past years. I tell her of Heber and the goats, of Anna, of my escalating frustrations, and lastly, in husky whisper, I tell her of Aaron.

Abigail's voice ceases to be that of the loud

87

hawker. "My dear friend, I am so sorry about your baby. To lose a child is a hurt unlike any other." For several seconds she cradles her knees while seeming to drift into some misplaced grief of her own.

"Stay with me," she directs, abruptly rising. "I'll be in this city for awhile yet. And need I remind you that you are the child and widow of merchants? It is proper that you work with me and learn your rightful trade."

It is futile to protest.

Abigail further elaborates upon my future. "You are uncommonly pretty. Your skin is too creamy, your lashes too long, and even your lips are too pink. And when you smile! Oh my, we don't need to add to our problems." With her hands resting on her hips she decides, "It is better for us if you continue to be a boy. Tell me, do you have a name for your boy-self?"

I flex my muscles. "Yes. My name is Mareshah."

Abigail laughs into her dirty hands. "Mareshah? All right, Mareshah it is. We'll explain to the curious that you are my nephew, recently arrived from Sebaste. Come, we can't leave that old man in charge of things too long." She pauses, again studying my appearance. "We'll need to dirty you a little more."

I think I am already quite soiled, but as we leave the house Abigail spots a pile of ashes. I yield to her urging and smear soot over my face, garments, and arms. Anna would declare the grimy results an overstatement. However, Abigail beams her approval. I look at my unkempt friend. We do appear related.

TWELVE

Undeniably merchandising is in my blood. My mentor, Abigail, odd in so many ways, proves very sane in teaching me the art of profitable sales.

During the slower hours we talk. Rather, it is I who talks in response to her ever-present questions. Abigail asks my views on everything from hair styles to politics. "All right, child, you say Palestine would be better off if Rome had never come to power. Well," she argues, "what about our Roman Peace? Surely you can't fault that."

I know she won't let me be until I answer. "Roman Peace is no different than if parents tied their children to separate trees, and then boasted, 'See how nicely our children get along. They just never fight.'" That is my opinion. I hope she doesn't mind.

Abigail covers her mouth and snickers. Sometimes she makes me feel quite clever.

No customers are about when Abigail suddenly announces, "Tonight we will not be going home. We'll be eating with friends."

What friends? I can't recall her mentioning being close to anyone, although some evenings she leaves me home alone so she can "do errands."

The sun is gone when we close shop. In the soft light of evening we follow the water's edge, stepping in the direction toward the shed I had first used for lodging.

"Where are we going?"

"I told you, to be with friends."

We proceed along the shore, sometimes across sandy stretches, sometimes over rocky beach. The moon is only a sliver. Clouds periodically move to hide even that slim light.

"We bathe now."

"Bathe?" *Abigail bathe?*

She cackles loudly. "Yes, here in the sea, here in the sea. Roman baths are warm and fragrant, but none offer the luxury of this water. Here, put your clothes by this rock. They will be easier to find in the dark."

We step into the gentle waves. I am disappointed that the sun has taken our light away, as I have never seen Abigail clean and can't begin to imagine how a wash might affect her. For several minutes we dip, splash, and scrub.

"Come," Abigail calls to me as she moves toward shore. "Please dress quickly." Dressing as Mareshah cannot be done quickly. However, she did say please, so I do my best.

This time, as we resume our travel, we leave the waterfront. Abigail says nothing. The only interruption of the night's quiet comes from a lone sea-bird. The clouds increase. Uneasiness fills my chest.

In this darkness I can barely discern a rise of land looming before us. We head straight toward it. "Give me your hand," orders Abigail. With her free hand she pushes aside tall grasses hindering our passing. "Stay close, child."

Total blackness engulfs us. Our clasped hands bump a wall of earth. I cry out.

"Hush!" warns Abigail.

I gasp, "Are we in a cave?"

"Yes."

At her insistence I am silent. But my heart's loud pounding cannot be stilled. An expanding terror creeps over me. Why has Abigail brought me here? Has she gone totally mad? Do I walk in the belly of the earth with a crazy woman?

Abigail's hand tightens its hold. The ground is rocky. We shuffle in the darkness going farther, farther . . . where? A faint light comes from some distant source. As we round a corner a wide passageway greets us. Projecting from these rough walls are four flaming torches. In their welcomed light I see a table and, nearby that, a couch.

Abigail drops my hand. Although damp hair hangs over her face, I know she is smiling. "Don't be afraid, dear. You are safe." She points to the couch. "Rest now, I will be back shortly."

Bewildered, I watch her move away and disappear behind a bend. Heeding her words, I collapse onto the couch. I run my fingers through my hair to hurry its drying.

The combination of moist hair, the cave's coolness, and these strange surroundings causes me to shiver. Then I spy a shawl draped over the other end of the couch. I wrap myself in its softness, grateful for the warmth.

The flickering torches cast shadows of grotesque butterflies about the grotto. Am I in an eerie dream? Or bewitched?

Oh, Anna, I wish you were here.

I close my eyes and again see green slopes and a little boy running, laughing. I ache to hold him and know his wet kisses. I am so weary, so spent, so . . . .

"Wake up," encourages a gentle voice.

Although startled from a nap, I do not jump. For I am spellbound. Above me stands a most beautiful woman. Her graying hair is styled high and accented with tiny beads shimmering in the amber glow of torch light. A long crimson gown drapes her lovely body. An armlet of gold, signifying authority, circles her skin.

"Who are you?" I hear myself ask.

She smiles. Even, white teeth complete her comliness.

"Who are you?" I repeat. "And where is Abigail?"

"You wish to see that crazy old woman?"

"I do." I rise to my feet to emphasize my wish, then grow timid. "Please."

"Marah, look at me."

I study this elegant lady who knows my name. It cannot be!

92

"Abigail? *Abigail!*"

"Yes, I am Abigail."

What can all this mean? I shiver now, not from chill or even fear. For I stand at the threshold of mystery and am willing to take the next step.

"Soon, dear Marah, all this will be explained. But first you must be made ready."

Abigail leads me into yet another tunnel. We pass beneath an archway supported by heavy beams and then enter a great cavern.

Torches abound on all walls bathing the area in light. The floor is covered with rugs of bright patterns. In the middle of the room stands a massive table composed of many boards. Flanking it are a host of colorful pillows. Standing about are people attired in finery.

Abigail speaks and they immediately attend her every word.

"My friend is joining us this evening. Would someone please prepare her."

A large woman with amber-brown eyes presents herself and escorts me to an ante-room. This chamber is supplied with jars, mounds of clothing, baskets filled with accessories, and a large piece of polished brass for reflecting. She swiftly removes the shepherd garb and offers me scented oils. Fascinated, I watch as this pleasant woman rummages through the many garments.

"This will do," she decides.

I am gowned in a dress of supple fabric the color of dry sand. She fastens a golden girdle about my waist. In moments her deft fingers brush and arrange my hair. She pulls back one side and secures it with a jeweled comb. From the pile of shoes she selects pretty sandals. My new friend announces me ready.

I inspect my reflection. This transformation is as marvelous as Abigail's.

We return to the others. New arrivals have joined with those now gathered at the great table. The talking ceases as Abigail rises to greet me.

"I approve," she says, smiling. "Friends, this is Helper." I bow in polite greeting, wondering when I will learn the meaning of this gathering and why I am included. Abigail spreads her slender arms, "These are my friends . . . Potter, Tentmaker, Carpenter, Teacher. . . ."

No one is called by given name, except Abigail.

She places me at her left. The seat to her right is vacant. Turning to me, Abigail asks, "Have you heard of Fabius the Delayer?"

I am bursting with questions and here she asks me if I know someone called Fabius. I stifle a scream. "No," I say, but look about in case he might be sitting nearby.

I hear muffled chuckles.

"Dear, he lived over 200 years ago. Fabius Maximus was the dictator of Rome during a time when Carthage threatened to conquer. Fabius believed the Roman troops, weary and discouraged from long battles, might recover to a position of strength if given enough time. Since he feared a war would only result in Rome's defeat, this dictator launched a campaign to irritate and weaken the Carthaginian might." Abigail pauses, waiting for my response.

"This is interesting," I allow, "but I don't

understand what it has to do with all this."

"We, too, face an enemy too strong to defeat," explains Abigail.

"An enemy?"

"That's right, an enemy. Rome is our foe, with her suffocating domination of Palestine. We here are a secret community pledged to follow Fabius's example and harass our adversary.

"While zealots openly rebel, we plant thorns beneath the foot of Rome. Until that day comes when we defend our homeland with a strong army, we content ourselves with making life difficult for our oppressor."

Is this possible? A secret fellowship bent on Rome's undoing, functioning beneath the very palace of Caesar's procurator?

I look at the lovely face that heretofore I had only seen screened by filth. "I . . . I am so confused. Not just by the daring of this group, but by you, Abigail. I've only known you as the dirty, loud, and somewhat odd merchant. And these past weeks I've lived and worked with you. The lady I talk with now is a stranger."

Abigail's eyes, accustomed to pulling hidden truths from me, beg me to realize her's. "For years I have been the crazy seller of the marketplace. In this disguise I am considered a little mad, and therefore harmless. Officials and soldiers openly discuss news and plans within my hearing."

She reaches for my hand. "Eleazor and your parents supported this cause."

Dumbfounded, I gasp, "They never told me anything of this."

"That was for your protection. If any trouble came, your words of innocence would hold the strength of truth."

Pieces of long forgotten conversations come to mind. "Yes, I do remember their speaking of you. I never understood the reason for their esteem."

The torches spill their golden radiance throughout the large chamber. However, the illumination I seek can only come from Abigail. "People have always supported causes and sacrificed for dreams," I begin, "and I heartily share your views for the liberation of our land. But what prompts you to pour out your energies to such an extreme for this cause?"

A stillness comes upon the assembled; not the hush of curious about to be satisfied, but of respect for the already known answer.

Abigail folds her hands on the table. She joins the others in the soundlessness of the moment. Looking at me, she says, "My mother was only twelve when she was raped." Abigail's frank words shock me. I glance at the others and read compassion on every face. Quickly I turn my attention back to her telling.

"For months fear and shame closed my mother's mouth. Eventually she told that a Roman nobleman was responsible for the new life she carried. No punishment came to him. But my poor mother suffered every day of her life for this assault. Lust resides in men of all nations, still I hated my unknown *Roman* father.

"Then in young womanhood I met Simon. He didn't care that I was half Roman. After we married we moved to Bethlehem. Our son, David, was a beautiful baby, always smiling. I thought it was the sunshine itself I had borne.

"Herod the Great was king at the time. He ruled with a cruel and shaky scepter, ever fearful that someone would steal his throne.

"One day Magi from the East traveled to Jerusalem inquiring after a newly born king of the Jews. Pretending interest, rather than revealing his panic, Herod called all the chief priests and scribes and asked where the Messiah was to be born. Citing the prophet Micah, they explained that Bethlehem was the favored city.

"Herod, feigning interest, urged the eastern visitors to let him know immediately when this new king was found so that he, too, might pay homage. The Magi never returned to Herod. Enraged over the slight, and horrified at the idea of a new king, Herod ordered the death of all little boys under two. Surely with that deed accomplished the threat would end."

Abigail covers her face with her hands. "The soldiers barged into our home and snatched David from his father's arms. While we watched in helpless outrage they unleashed Roman power upon his baby flesh. My Simon died of grief a short while later.

"I cannot bring back their lives, nor the lives of all the little ones slaughtered that day in and around Bethlehem. I vow, however, to wound, hinder, and someday defeat the powers responsible!"

I recall my own grief. Goats are only beasts and act as such. But for men to willfully murder children . . . truly this subjugation must end! I am eager to support this cause.

I touch her hand and speak my sympathy. Then I inquire, "Do all these people also know pain from the hand of Rome?"

"They do. We are here to do what we can to topple Caesar's throne. Our hope, dear, is that you will help in our cause."

"What do you want me to do?"

Abigail smiles and is the fairer for it. "How pleased Eleazor and your parents would be! Soon we will eat and then we will discuss plans and plots. As soon as Doctor arrives we will begin."

"Doctor?"

"Yes, a countryman who holds even Rome's trust."

THIRTEEN

"At last we may eat!" cheers the stocky man called Carpenter. I look up to see two newcomers enter. One, tall and hooded, follows a slightly bent, white-haired gentleman. The older man stops at the far end of the table. After a considered reshaping and fluffing of the cushion he drops upon it with a large sigh of pleasure. His face is kind and exudes merriment. This must be the esteemed doctor! My attention is so upon him that I give little notice to the other man proceeding to the empty seat next to Abigail.

"Agreed," declares our hostess, "we eat."

Even Anna would be hard put to spread such a table. Mounded upon finely crafted brass trays are almonds, pomegranates, grapes, and to my delight, apples. I laugh over the unexpected elegance of cheese when served from graceful platters. Carpenter leads the applause for the roasted lamb. Breads and wine come from a seemingly unending supply. I am glad to be so hungry.

"How did all this food get here?" I ask Abigail.

"We all bring what we can. Our cooks manage the distribution." I assume by her brief, whispered answer that this isn't the time for further questions.

The feast is only beginning when the white-haired man calls to Abigail, "Who is the beautiful addition?" He smiles warmly at me. I sense an appreciative blush rushing to my face.

Abigail laughs and shakes her fist at him. "I knew it would be only minutes before you noticed her. This is Helper. Be nice, she is only a child." To me she teasingly cautions, "And that old rooster is known as the Sweeper."

He rises and bows low. "At last loveliness graces our table." I return his bow and thank him.

Abigail nudges me. "Please meet our Doctor. He is handsomer than Sweeper, and of course, much brighter." I catch her wink directed toward the far end of the table.

So this tall one is Doctor. Mildly amused by my mistake, I turn to greet the honored one at Abigail's right. The man's large hands grasp the edges of his hood to draw it back.

Stupefied, I stifle a cry.

Joel!

Joel is Doctor! Calling upon some hidden strength, I manage a casual, "I'm happy to meet you, sir." He smiles politely and resumes eating and chatting with our leader. *He doesn't even recognize me!*

I do my best to focus upon the meal. However, memories of Abner, the sheep, Caesarea, the Great Sea . . . and now the physical presence of Joel. . . .

I am startled from my musings by a quick hug from Abigail. "Yes, I've known this girl from her birth."

"And you are the richer for it, I'm sure." Joel studies me for a moment. "Tell me, young Helper, something about yourself."

I want to tell him we once laughed and walked and worked together. Instead, I smile and say, "There is little to mention."

And so we discuss the food and sip the wine. Suddenly he pulls the candlestick closer to me, in order that he might scrutinize my face.

Then he blurts, "I know we've met, but where?"

I look at him with all the innocence I can muster and sweetly accuse, "If that is so, then I am offended that you do not remember me." Turning to my left, I ask for more bread, please.

Abigail whispers to me, "Has he met you before, dear?" Before I can even start my answer, Joel stands to pace about the chamber. By now others are staring at him, as though by collective concentration they might jar Joel's thoughts into remembering.

I wish to let him fret a little more, but I cannot contain my mirth. Giggles erupt. I rise from the table hoping to make an exit while I still own dignified conduct. But it is too late. Outrageous laughter overtakes me. Joel, who is standing, hastens to my side and attempts to calm me.

An absolute hush covers the room. Every eye is upon me as Joel does his best to bring my outburst to an end. When I do manage control, Joel demands an explanation. Mindful that names are not used, I whisper my words to him. "Joel, I am Mareshah!"

He staggers back, "That dirty shepherd boy?"

"Yes, that dirty shepherd boy."

His laughter is instant and contagious. It is now my turn to do some explaining to a very puzzled Abigail and these new friends.

I tell of my disguise designed to give me protection during my trip to Caesarea, but I say nothing of the events leading to that journey.

Abigail claps her hands. "Imagine, my dear Doctor, you the high master of disguises, fooled by our young guest."

Joel rubs his chin, sits down, and sheepishly responds, "I can't imagine that I was so completely deceived. I honestly thought her to be a boy. This news explains much about that young shepherd. He had a very strange loping walk and an unusual voice. You know, I thought him to be kind of a sissy. He wouldn't even take a dip in the river with me." Joel covers his face with his hands and groans.

I find his embarrassment charming. However, to ease his plight, I change the subject.

"So you are a physician? I understand now how you were such a help to injured Abner."

Abner!

"Is Abner also a member of the cause?"

Joel grins and admits, "He is." After a quick drink, Joel wipes his mouth with the back of his hand. "You'll soon learn his part." Rising to his feet, Joel announces, "Please everyone, listen to my words.

"Friends, as you know, we of the Fabius Cause enjoy the protection of this cave. Other patriots have no such shelter and face greater risk when they gather.

"On a recent visit to Sebaste I learned of three zealots, already convicted of treason, needing help. They had escaped from the hand of Rome several weeks ago and now were in hiding at the Old Inn of Sebaste. The problem came about when several soldiers came to the inn. If the zealots were recognized by these soldiers, their lives would be shortly over. Rome wanted their deaths." Joel pales and his voice chokes, "Crucifixion is ugly."

I cringe. Father once described to me the agonies of this death. Not even a mad dog should endure such a fate.

Joel continues, "But along came Abner to the rescue. He managed to work his way into the inn's kitchen . . . and improved the wine."

Turning to me, Joel clarifies why everyone is chuckling. "Abner studies potions. I bring him powders, herbs, and medicines. He uses these to brew irritants for Rome. All his concoctions are stored in his house. That's why he put us in the other buildings."

Again Joel addresses the group. "Abner added something to the wine which produced an immediate skin rash. Long before dawn the wine-bibbing soldiers were frantically scratching their new itches.

"Disguised as a Greek nobleman, I then entered the inn. A nearby soldier cursed his skin condition. I offered to examine his mottled arm, then told him, 'I saw a skin condition like that in Greece. If untreated it turns into leprosy.' The poor soldier moaned, 'What can be done to help us?' I calmed him by telling him of a wise physician, a Jew, working in Caesarea. . . ."

The audience breaks into laughter.

Joel brings us again to his story. "After I left the inn I headed for Abner's place. Abner stayed behind and alerted the zealots that confusion might soon occur among the Roman troops, making escape possible. He was right. The distressed soldiers begged to be sent back to Caesarea for treatment. While their chief officer considered this request, Abner started home.

"As he neared his destination, racing horses bearing the frantic soldiers tore past him. One of the Roman mounts kicked up a rock, injuring Abner. Our new friend here, posing as a shepherd boy, happened by and kindly aided the old man." He smiles warmly down at me and I tingle with a strange joy.

The assembled lift their ever-filled goblets and praise my deed. Flustered by their attention, I stammer my thanks, then turn quickly back to the food before me.

"By the way," Joel comments, "I did see those soldiers after I returned to Caesarea. I applied a paste and told them not to drink wine for a month. To their amazement and joy the rash eased and the grateful army paid a nice fee." Joel places a bag of coins on the table. "For the freedom of Palestine," he intones. "For the freedom of Palestine," they echo.

This night of unbelievable events ends too soon. Abigail rises and we clasp arms while she commends the courage of the gathered. After invoking the blessings of the Lord God, she dismisses us.

A few leave at a time. "It lessens the chance of detection," she explains.

The table is cleared of all banquet traces. Only a scant number of people remain, when Abigail unfastens her armlet and rubs the slight indenting of her skin. "Are your questions all satisfied?" she queries me.

"Some are. But I've been wondering how you ever found this cave?"

"I didn't, Carpenter did. He was walking his dog early one evening when a rat scurried by. The dog took chase, with Carpenter right behind. Startled by something, he stopped and listened. It was the sound of his dog's barking . . . it echoed. Cautiously he neared the sound and found his dog in a cave. Carpenter retrieved his pet, then marked the entrance with a small arrangement of stones. Before dawn Carpenter returned with a bucket of coals and a torch.

"After careful study Carpenter believed the labyrinth to be safe, hidden, and unknown to anyone. Exactly what we needed for our growing number to use for a meeting place.

"Putting his building skills to work, he constructed a small shed that would both hide and identify the entrance. Carpenter explained to the patrolling soldiers that his wife ousted him sometimes and he needed the shack for occasional shelter. Amused by this tale of domestic strife, they let Carpenter putter about in peace."

Joel interrupts, "Remember the beach shed you stayed in that night? That was Carpenter's shack."

Learning to handle surprises, I calmly ask, "Were you meeting here that evening?"

"Some of us were. On the second night as we came to meet, my hood caught on the loose board of the shed. I feared you might be awake, but then I heard awful snoring . . ." he teases.

"So you were the rat I heard."

Abigail reminds us it is time to leave. "We must change garments and become our other selves."

I touch my soft gown and wonder if ever again I shall be so clothed.

Joel and Sweeper offer to escort us home. Sweeper grandly lifts Abigail's arm. "We always have to help her back. Poor thing gets lost so easily."

Heavy coastal fog hugs the beach. Joel takes my hand and tucks it into the warmth of his bent arm. We follow the shore line, walking behind Abigail and Sweeper.

"I hope you aren't angry with me for being Mareshah," I ask.

"I am. But forgiveness is offered if you tell me your real name."

"I thought given names weren't to be shared."

"For the most part they are not. Abigail's, of course, is known." He pulls me away from an advancing wave. "If any of us are ever arrested we

106

cannot be forced to disclose that which in truth we do not know. Caesarea has many carpenters. . . . If the authorities needed to find Carpenter, they'd have a big search.

"But I'd like to call you something other than Helper. Go ahead and ask Abigail if you may tell me."

"It's Marah," I tell him. I don't need to get her permission for everything.

"Marah." He pats my hand. "I like it."

We walk in silence. The streets of the city are hushed. We pass a beggar dozing in a doorway. A cat pursuing a small rat glares at us for hindering his hunt.

Abigail and Sweeper reach our doorway, then turn and wait for us. We stop short. Joel drops my hand. "I look forward to seeing you again, Marah."

Silver mists wrap around this rare moment. I remember every second we spent at Abner's, guiding sheep, everything.

"Joel?"

He stands here before me, tall, handsome and very near. I can't resist. I whack his back.

FOURTEEN

Abigail will not allow her market space to be neat. She is convinced that the gods of trade bless clutter. Nevertheless, I try to bring some hint of harmony out of today's wares of boxes, bracelets, stools, shawls, cushions, and oranges.

Abigail returns from wherever she has been with her arms full of colorful mats. Noticing my efforts toward neatness, she scowls and mutters, "Chaos is the best condition for my shop." With that she tosses everything once again into disarray. I join in the wild deorganization until we drop with laughter.

It is only moments later when I hear Abigail yelling, "If you aren't going to buy, don't keep handling the shawls!" I see that a man in the white toga of Roman citizenship is Abigail's target.

"I would buy, old woman, but the price you ask is nothing short of robbery!"

Abigail waves her arms. "The shawl you hold is perfectly woven. If you are too dull to know its worth, go to the dogs!" She spits for emphasis.

The Roman accepts her challenge. They contest long and hard over price. At length Abigail throws her hands skyward, despairing over the poverty this man wishes to foist upon her. "All right, take the shawl at your price and be off!" she shrieks. Pleased with his cunning, the Roman pushes his bargaining further and asks for three more shawls, all to be priced equal with the first.

Abigail shakes her fist and screams, "You sons of Caesar are all thieves! Take the shawls and leave my sight!"

We watch the Roman disappear into the crowd smirking over his cleverness.

"Abigail, you trickster! That man paid more than you sold the same shawl for this morning. What's more, you sold him four!"

She looks at me with wide, guileless eyes, "Oh, how awful of me."

I accuse, "Your disguise also increases sales." This odd woman of the marketplace is not shamed one morsel by my scoldings. Abigail rests her hands upon her hips, rolls her eyes, and in sultry voice murmurs, "My costume does even more, my dear, it protects my virtue. I haven't found a man yet eager to sleep with a filthy, demented woman."

I have to giggle over her inventive scheme, but just the same I am bothered by her dealings. Stealing, deception, cheating cannot be right. Yet this woman is completely convinced that in fighting Rome, anything and everything is fair. I am troubled within, but the pricks of my own conscience plague me enough without adding the misdeeds of another to my worries.

I survey Abigail's begrimed person, and remember her other self, so beautiful, elegant, womanly. And an unanswered question comes to mind.

"Abigail, the fine clothes of the cave . . . how did you get them?"

"They belong to us."

"But they look so costly!"

"They are, they are." She pauses, assuring herself that no unwelcome ears are near. "You, I, all of Palestine pay heavily for every garment. It is our tax money that clothes Rome. Choice items are imported for the procurator and his household. We meet most incoming ships. Many of the goods we manage to . . . ah, claim. As we wear the finery we remind ourselves of what we in truth own."

She shakes her already disheveled hair and chuckles, "Sometimes to fatten the purse of our cause, I sell some of the articles right here back to the Romans."

A coming festival to celebrate the glories of Rome will provide an excellent opportunity to embarrass our conquerors.

One night in the cave, Sweeper announces that the hippodrome is to house the event. All manner of races are to take place. Following these contests, special dancers from the city of Rome itself will perform. Then a great trumpet salute to praise Tiberius Caesar will conclude the affair.

Koydal, the tailor, is to design costumes for these trumpeters. He boasts of this assignment from Rome to everyone he meets. We of the cause give consideration to his announcement.

"Since it is the trumpets we wish to reach," begins our leader, Abigail, "and since Koydal seems our best channel to those horns, and since you, Marah, are a skilled seamstress, we offer you the opportunity to serve our mission." I am honored. I accept the challenge.

Later that evening I remind Abigail that I have already met Koydal. She adds more wine to her almost empty cup. "The man is a womanizer all right. That is, unless he hears the mention of his wife, Martha. Koydal is terrified of her. Remember that and you'll be quite safe."

I find Koydal wrapped in folds of new material. Lifting his whiskered chin, he peers down at me. "Ahh, lovely lady, you have returned. How may I help you?"

"I understand that you are to sew the costumes for the trumpet players."

"Yes, yes, a large order given to the city's finest tailor."

I smile and demurely say, "I need employment. With such a big task facing you, surely you could use help."

Koydal unwraps himself and once more surveys my frame. I find him disgusting.

"What is your name, my lovely one?"

"Marah."

"Marah . . . 'bitter,' I believe."

I nod, "Yes, it means that."

"Perhaps we might sweeten it, dear lady." He strokes my arm, allowing his hand to linger. For the sake of Palestine, I smile.

"The fabric I held will be used for the garments. We need to make twelve outfits." He shows me the pattern. "It is a simple design, long sleeves, with a center back seam. Very handsome, don't you think?"

We work long past dusk and finish three outfits.

"Well," probes Abigail, "how pushy was Koydal?"

"He tries to be overly friendly." I smile with the remembering. "But today his Martha came in. She is really very beautiful with fierce eyes. When she is near, Koydal loses his wayward interests. After her visit, if Koydal looked too long at me I had only to say, 'Is that Martha coming down the street?' and the once-lustful man would jump back to sew feverishly."

Abigail and I exchange random news over our supper of fish and bread. She wipes the corners of her mouth and casually asks, "Tell me what you think of Joel?"

"What do you mean?"

Now her tone loses all casualness. "Marah, what do you think of Joel?"

"He seems very nice."

Abigail squints her eyes. "Is that all?"

"Oh, Abigail, of course, he is without question the handsomest man I've ever seen. And I've enjoyed his company since that day I met him at Abner's. Now, does that satisfy you?"

"A little," she admits, "a little."

Koydal's broom obediently stirs the floor's dust and scraps. "After today's work the costumes for the trumpeters will be finished." True to Koydal's prediction, the garments are splendid. "Every eye will be on the trumpeters," he boasts. I smile and comment, "I certainly hope so."

The thin man rests his broom against the wall. "The outfits need to be at the hippodrome by morning."

This is the word I have waited for these long days of sewing. "You must be very weary, sir, let me make the arrangements."

"I am not in the least tired," protests Koydal, straightening his shoulders in proof of his manly endurance. "But the procurator's wife sent an emergency plea for a new gown. She expected a shipment of garments from Rome, but something must have happened to them in transit. So now, in less than four days, I am to design a fashion masterpiece." Again he sighs.

I feel a moment of compassion for this man. "Oh sir, without a doubt you'll present her with a dress far lovelier than Rome ever could."

He agrees, then adds, "I appreciate your offer to get these garments to the hippodrome. Please do take care of it." My employer then hands me a small cloth pouch. "Your salary, my lovely lady." As usual his eyes caress my body, but he makes no move to touch me. I am grateful for the amazing protection derived from the mentioning of Martha.

Koydal unfolds the last of the outfits and as he begins the finishing work he bids me leave to do the assigned task.

I hurry through the masses of the marketplace to the shop of Sandalmaker. A family is buying shoes for their two children. Sandalmaker spots me and is eager to hear my news. But a sale is important too. We exercise prudence. I browse through his basket of thongs and he announces he will serve me shortly. Soon we are alone. "Koydal wants the costumes transported by tomorrow."

"Good! I've just learned that the trumpets arrived from Rome and are to be moved from the dock to the hippodrome sometime this morning. The timing couldn't be better. I'll be at Koydal's about sunset. Tell him to expect me."

I decide to be Mareshah for this task. Young boys often do night errands and wouldn't attract the attention a woman might.

The sky is spread with the last splendor of sunset when Sandalmaker loads the costumes into his cart. I join him a short ways from Koydal's shop and help escort the rumbling wagon along the bumpy road.

We are permitted entrance to the storeroom of the hippodrome, holding the many items needed for the coming celebration. The latest arrivals, the long trumpets, rest in front of the other supplies.

Their absence would be immediately noticed. Sandalmaker calls to the guard. "These horns

114

are in danger of being banged about. Do you mind if we move them out of the way?" The guard, apparently weary of protecting the contents of this storeroom, drones, "Do what suits you, man."

As we empty Sandalmaker's cart of the clothes, we refill the space with shining instruments, until all are safely hidden beneath a canvas.

Night screens our moves. We are coming upon Abigail's house when from a bush springs a large figure. He rushes for the cart. "I'll take your cargo, whatever it may be!" He curses and shoves Sandalmaker to the ground. These trumpets cannot be lost! I pound my fists upon the intruder's back while a dazed Sandalmaker tries to rise.

The robber growls, "Get out of my way, boy. This is a contest between men!" He hits my face so hard that my head covering falls off and my knotted hair loosens. As I grope for a nearby stick, he begins kicking my back. . . .

"Marah, are you all right?" It is Abigail hovering over me. "How are you feeling?" I look around. I am in Abigail's house. I hurt in every part of body.

"You took quite a clobbering, my friend," says Sandalmaker. "But while you held that villain's interest I gave him a good whack with a trumpet. Didn't even dent the horn, but he will be dreaming a good while longer, I wager."

"Where are the trumpets?"

"They're here . . . awaiting our touch. We'll keep them hidden until just before the event.

Then the trumpets will be "found" at the last minute, giving the musicians no time to warm up or practice." Sandalmaker's words cause Abigail to laugh. I laugh too, in spite of my aches.

From Sandalmaker's plump basket come the many strips of thin leather. Abigail brings out the pot of glue and by daylight the deed is done.

The day of celebration dawns with the bright beauty of a typical Caesarean day. Many important officials have already arrived, eager to be seen and applauded. There is an air of high excitement throughout the city, for this is the day to rejoice in the glory of Caesar.

Only occasionally do we of the cause get to see the immediate results of our labors. We learn of rescues, of prisoners fed, of the needy receiving our aid. Yes, we hear of the many nippings at the heel of Rome. But a public witness of our efforts is a rare sight. This day is to be a day of exception.

We scatter ourselves throughout the vast audience. I rely on my veil to hide my bruises. The events begin. The dancers dip and stretch like vines in a summer breeze, then lastly bow before the booth of the high officials.

I find the races so enthralling that I almost forget our purpose in coming. As the contests end, I tense in expectation of the final event.

The honored trumpeters parade before us, holding aloft their shining, newly found horns. The crowd voices a unified, "Ahh!" of approval. Koydal was correct, every eye is upon them. They stand before the procurator and raise the trumpets to their lips. A hush fills the stadium. The grandly attired musicians tilt back their heads and with proud force blow the horns in salutation.

But the clear song of trumpet comes not. For high into each horn there are secured thin strips of leather. When blown, the sound produced is like that vulgar noise made by vibrating the tongue between the lips.

The audience, supporters of Rome and dissenters alike, are caught for an instant in the pure stillness similar to the lull before a storm. And that storm does come. First in the winds of isolated guffaws, followed by a torrent of wild, uncontrolled laughter.

We of the cause concur with the trumpets' statement of tribute to the glories and greatness of Caesar and his Rome.

FIFTEEN

I wish she would stop. But no, she bombards me with her continuous comments and questions. "My, how handsome Joel is this evening. . . . What superb leadership he gives the cause. . . . Do you see how Joel smiles at you?"

"Abigail, please," I futilely implore.

The hours spent serving the market's demands pass. Dusk brushes shades of crimson across sky and sea. Perhaps this artistry of the Creator reminds Abigail of other things. For as we walk to the meeting her words hold no mention of Joel.

"You know, Marah, our cause does more than irritate Rome and protect patriots."

"I know that charity is done among the needy of Palestine."

"We also preserve the treasures of Palestine."

The cave is quiet this evening. Only a few of

the torches challenge the darkness. A small supper is shared by the half dozen of us who gather. We eat in leisure and then clear the table. I am curious about the business at hand since it is not our usual night to meet. Teacher lights the remaining torches. No one speaks during the ceremony. With the new brightness comes a sense of expectancy. I partake of it, but have no idea what we are about to do.

Joel and Sweeper approach the wide cabinet. Is it my imagination or do their hands tremble as they remove the large scroll and place it on the table? Joel smiles as though he owns some grand news. He turns to me.

"Rome allows us to worship the Lord God, to read our Scriptures, and to teach their precepts." This isn't exactly news to me. I wait for his further comments. "There are those who fear our holy writings and mean to destroy them. So we borrow sacred scrolls from the synagogues, make copies, then hide the reproductions here in the cave."

Abigail joins Joel and Sweeper as they unroll the parchment. A wave of awkwardness comes over me; I am the only Samaritan present.

"Samaritan scriptures," I point out, "consist of only the books of Moses." My words don't seem to upset anyone, so I continue, "I believe you Jews have more . . . prophets, history, and poetry. . . . Isn't that correct?"

Joel smoothes the scroll, then beckons to me. "You are right. Here in our community of the cause we don't make distinctions between Jew and Samaritan. However, we do honor the whole of Hebrew writings as a precious treasure. And as such we protect it.

"Come, see what we copy tonight. It is from the collection of the Psalms. King David tended sheep as a youth. In this poem he speaks of God as his shepherd."

"Really?" I am not thrilled by the image.

"Please read the psalm, Marah." Joel's moist eyes amplify the request of his words.

I am nervous. I am also an educated woman, and . . . well, Joel did ask so nicely. I pick up the scroll and read,

> The Lord is my shepherd, I shall lack
>   nothing.
> He makes me lie down in green pastures,
> he leads me beside quiet waters,
>   he restores my soul.
> He guides me in paths of righteousness
>   for his name's sake.
> Even though I walk
>   through the valley of the shadow of
>   death,
> I will fear no evil,
>   for you are with me;
> your rod and your staff,
>   they comfort me.
>
> You prepare a table before me
>   in the presence of my enemies.
> You anoint my head with oil;
>   my cup overflows.

Surely goodness and love will follow me
  all the days of my life,
and I will dwell in the house of the Lord
  forever.

The simple passage stirs my imagination and an unrecognized something deep within me. Could that be so? God, the Lord God, a shepherd . . . a shepherd dedicated to his sheep? Is he really eager to lavish tender care upon his flock, upon *me?*

I place the scroll back on the table. Pointing to it I ask Joel, "Is that how you see God?"

"Yes."

Joel and Sweeper often come to our house. I have learned that Joel is second, under Abigail, in command of the cause. They have much to discuss. Sweeper's presence is never explained, but Abigail clearly is pleased to see him. I busy myself with tidying things as the three of them visit. I try not to overly notice Joel.

Yet there he sits. Perfect to look upon. A delight to ponder. Our handsome guest moves his head to one side, causing his black curls to sway ever so slightly. I want to smooth them and feel their softness. Instead I shake out the newly laundered clothes. Some items, I notice, have need of mending. Tomorrow I will do that task. I can mend garments. Joel mends people.

As a physician, Joel tends the aches and injuries of the citizenry of Caesarea. The Jewish sector of this city feels a special ownership of him. Abigail says that Rome, too, appreciates Joel's skill. Once he aided the procurator's favorite mare in a difficult delivery of twin foals. With that event, Rome almost made him a god.

Joel is also gifted in bringing healing to weary spirits. To the discouraged within our cause he counsels, "We may be in Rome's rule, but here in the cave we know we are sovereign citizens of our homeland. Someday we will openly claim what is our own!"

I fold the last garment and decide that Joel is above all other men. But I must end these musings. It is not right that I savor these feelings. I resolve to work harder for Abigail, do more in the cause, finish the mending . . .

"Marah," Abigail calls, snapping to order the clutter of my rambling thoughts. "Please, dear, entertain Joel for a while. Sweeper and I have to do an errand."

Oh, Abigail, not now! I help her with her cloak and tell her to please hurry back.

Joel is sprawled atop his favorite cushion, supporting his chin with his right fist. With his other hand he scratches a spot on the rug.

"Would you like something more to eat?" I offer.

"No," he half grins, "just some company."

I sit stiffly on the sofa opposite him.

Again he smiles, this time broadly.

"Marah, Mareshah . . ." he teases me as I still wear today's disguise, "whoever it is that you are, I've looked forward all day to seeing you. But then, in my thoughts all day I have seen you."

For one blissful moment I allow my eyes to enjoy his. Our words need to take a different route.

"Joel, I'm curious. How is it that you, a Jew, living in a Samaritan province, direct an effort to undo Rome?"

"I guess you've a right to know." Joel bunches the pillow under his chest, holding it with clasped hands.

"One day my father got into a heated argument with a Roman centurion. They quarreled over the comparative strengths of Rome and Greece. Father, part Greek himself, unwisely pointed out that while the Roman's ancestors were scarcely learning to be civilized, his were studying philosophy and the arts. He also mentioned that Jews were stronger of soul than Romans. Infuriated, the centurion brought charges against my father for slandering Rome.

"I was too young to understand what was taking place, but I do remember being frightened by the men with the breastplates and frowns.

"Friends carried my father home that day. His back was mangled and raw. He had fallen victim of the thirty-nine lashes. Infection set in and a fever burned. Mother tended his wounds and did her best to soothe him. I crouched in the corner and begged all the gods I'd ever heard about to spare his life.

"It was a cloudy afternoon when Father called us to his bedside. He told us never to give in to the bullying of tyrants and to take good care of each other. We watched as his thrashing forever stilled."

Joel sighs. "Of course our grief was enormous. Mother never recovered from the sorrow. She died before the year ended."

"Did you have family to take care of you?"

"No, no one. I was befriended by a dirty old hawker, new to the Jerusalem marketplace." He smiles, then sits up. "I guess you've met her."

Now I understand the bond between Abigail and Joel. He replaced her slain child. She is mother to him.

"Does Abigail work the markets in Jerusalem anymore?"

"At holy seasons, she often does."

We become lighthearted as we talk of the enterprising Abigail.

Joel looms into all my thoughts. I order myself not to yearn so for this man. I avoid being alone with him, except as he slips into my hidden dreams.

My head is throbbing, so Abigail goes to the meeting without me. I hope the evening of quiet will help the turmoil of my mind. I curl upon the low couch and begin the nightly practice of brushing my hair.

A demanding knock ends my brief peace.

I unbar the door.

"Joel! I thought you'd be at the meeting."

"Well, I'm not. May I come in?"

I don't answer, but he walks in anyway and drops to his usual cushion. I stand at the still-open door, brushing the ends of a handful of hair.

"Come in," he suggests.

I comply.

"Do you mind that I've come to visit when Abigail is away?"

I shake my head no.

He sits, wordlessly smiling at me. I take a seat on the couch and again brush my hair. Still he is silent.

"Well?"

"Well, I need to talk with you, Marah. Lately I find myself in a sweet torment that I am no longer able to squelch. I care so much about you."

"Do you even know enough about me to care?" Oh, why am I so rude? I try to undo my words. "Joel, you are a Jew, I am a Samaritan." Oh dear, I am messing this up the more.

"You know that matters nothing to me. I find you kind, wise, and very beautiful."

He starts toward me, but I lift my hand, cautioning him not to come near.

"What is it, Marah? What is this wall you build between us? I don't mean just tonight, but the barrier I feel you are always raising?"

I lower my eyes, my pain refuses to allow me to see his.

"Joel, I am married."

There is silence—a heavy, hurting silence. At last I look at him.

"Married?"

"Twice in fact."

I blurt out my life's happenings. I tell him of my parents, of Eleazor, of Heber and the goats, and of dear Aaron. And as usual, I cry.

Joel is many things, leader, doctor, teacher . . . he is also friend. He holds my hand as a friend would to comfort a friend.

"Marah, I need to think upon what you have

told me. My feelings remain, but I need to think."

After he leaves I resume my task of brushing away my hair's tangles. If only there were some way to brush away life's tangles.

"The sea is flat, business is dull, and my feet hurt. That is why I don't want to talk!" But Abigail, with that all-knowing manner of hers, peers into my soul and knows I am lying.

"Could it be that you miss all that herding?" she chides.

I glare at her and hold my tongue. She pats my arm. "It is over, dear. Live the life of now."

"Abigail, I'm married. In spite of everything, that is so."

"Do you plan to return to Heber?"

"No! Never, never." Yet my Samaritan heritage holds me bound to that union.

Abigail drops her hands to her sides. "Your life of then is done! All that went before is over. Today you live for the cause."

Can her words undo yesterday? Will I ever be free from Heber? I am unsettled by memories of his harshness, scowls, and goats. I remember that day. . . . *Oh, Aaron! My little boy!*

Abigail's arguments find growing response in me. "The old is finished, dear. You no longer are of Sebaste. You are of Palestine, the free Palestine. The free Marah."

I ache for the reality of her words.

Abigail and I are eating our evening meal when we hear the familiar knock at the door.

"Joel! Come in and share our supper," she invites. "We didn't expect you tonight."

He greets us, inquires after our health, and helps himself to the plate of lamb. We exchange pleasant banter for the next hour. At last he announces, "I didn't come for business, Abigail, or even supper. I came to ask a pretty lady to go for a walk with me."

"Oh, I'm sorry Joel, but I can't go. You might as well take Marah."

Her jesting doesn't amuse me.

"I, I really ought to do that mending."

"Nonsense!" argues Abigail, handing me a cape. "It is a lovely evening for a walk." She opens the door. "Smell that sweet air. It is the air of free people . . . *free* people, Marah."

Joel offers his arm. I hesitate, then accept it. He places his other hand over mine. I feel his strength and my increasing weakness.

The yellow lamplight, spilling out of the homes we pass, seems to beckon and invite. A deep aloneness comes over me. Not since Eleazor's death have I felt I really belonged to anyone.

"The stars hang close to the city tonight."

I agree, they do.

"I thought you might like to see the theater facing the sea. Once I promised a dirty shepherd boy that I'd show it to him."

Distant laughter, barking dogs, and birds not yet settled for sleep fill the night with sounds of life. Varied blooms perfume the coastal air. The stars and full moon offer sufficient light to ensure the safety of our steps.

"There it is, the theater."

"Is it all right for us to just walk in?"

"I'm sure it is. In fact there must be an edict enforcing it," he proclaims.

High in the stadium's arc we find seats. All seats do indeed oppose the sea. The dark blue waters reflect the stars and moon. I find the beauty of the view enhanced by the man at my side.

"I wish that sight were mine to give you."

"But you have," I whisper.

We sit in silence. It is enough to be together. Then he asks, "Did you ever love Heber?"

"No, but I tried to. I did love Eleazor. He was a fine man."

"That's what Abigail tells me."

Again we slip into silence. And again it is Joel who breaks it. "I never considered marriage. I always thought my life was destined to be limited to serving the cause.

"Marah, please pay close attention to my words. See how the sky is mirrored in the sea? We know the moon and stars hang in the heavens. Yet they appear to be in the sea as well. The water does not hold the lights, we see only an illusion.

"Rome has swallowed us. But our true habitation no more belongs to Rome than the moon and stars do to the sea. Someday the Messiah will come and liberate us. Until then we work to sour the belly of Rome."

He turns to face me. "Abigail is our leader. I honor her wisdom. She says our dream is our reality. The cave represents our homeland. All that you and I once were must be abandoned . . . Heber . . . my past . . . everything. We are citizens of a new realm. In that way we serve Palestine."

He outlines my chin with his forefinger. "Marah, my Marah. I love you."

I forget the sea, moon, stars, and even Palestine.

"With all my pleading I ask you to be my wife . . . together we will uphold the cause."

I want to say, "yes." I yearn to say, "yes." Instead, "But what of my marriage to. . . ."

He clasps his hand over my mouth. My great longing for Joel hushes any further protest from my fatigued conscience.

Never have I desired anyone, anything as I do this man. I start to speak my love, but this time he quiets me with his lips. Our kiss is sweet, sensual, and about to be repeated.

SIXTEEN

It is permitted. Boys are allowed, no, expected to
race and shout in the streets. As Mareshah, I take
full advantage of that privilege. But as Marah, I
content myself to merely sing my elation.

Joel loves me! Do you hear, oh earth and sky?
Joel and Marah are betrothed!

Abigail is delighted over our soon union. "Our
cause can only be strengthened by such cou-
pling." She also insists that wedding details
belong to her. "I've never had a child to marry
off. So you two relax and let me enjoy myself."

I can't relax. For into my pleasure charges the
accusing finger of guilt. I argue with myself.

*"It doesn't matter what Abigail declares, you
are yet lawful wife of Heber!"*

"But our marriage was so awful!"

*"You walked out on your husband. Do you
now only laugh it off?"*

"I do not laugh!"

"I heard you sing and laugh this very day."

I flee from my prosecutor. I *will* live these prenuptial days in a land of rainbowed bliss, in a garden of fresh joys. No guilt dare attack me in my walled paradise.

Two shabbily dressed youngsters approach our market displays. Abigail hurries toward them while I await her usual dictate, "Be off with you!" But there are no such orders. The children speak quietly with her. Then Abigail fills a basket with fruit and the very bread of our lunch. She places several coins in the hands of the taller child and hugs the little one.

"Rome has imprisoned their father," explains Abigail. I am forced to see that, even in my land of bliss, suffering for others continues.

"Abigail, most of what I once owned became Nabod's. However, when I left, Anna gave me a full purse. Perhaps it is appropriate to donate that money to our cause as a kind of dowry."

Abigail stares after the two children. "It would be very appropriate."

Tonight, even with the remembering of my charity, I still hear the waning cries of my sin.

Day is dissolving into evening when Abigail and I arrive at the cave. We go right away to the grotto where the garments are stored. Three of our women greet us. "Adorn her to be a fitting bride for our Doctor," instructs Abigail.

A large vessel filled with warm, scented water awaits. I soak, scrub, and rejoice. The ladies supply me with soft cloths for drying. A series of warmed towels draws the moisture from my washed hair. These friends are determined that I look my best. I obey their cheery command and smooth the fragrant cream over my clean skin.

Abigail has so ruled this event that I have not even seen my wedding dress. She holds it up now for my approval. I gasp. Surely the sky must be missing a piece of its loveliest blue.

"It is silk, dear," informs Abigail. "The procurator's wife ordered it for that festival at the hippodrome, but somehow it got misplaced." Could Abigail have had this very occasion in mind when she "happened to find" this exquisite gown?

All attention is focused upon my hair. How is it to be fashioned? One giggling friend proposes we comb it over my face. Another joins the merriment with the suggestion, "Let's make one long braid so your husband will be able to pull you easily about."

Then Abigail studies my head. "Her hair shall hang loose." From a silver tray holding an array of flowers, the ladies select tiny white blooms and secure them about my thoroughly brushed locks.

Pleased at last with their efforts, my attendants lead me to the mirror. I cannot believe the woman reflected is truly me. I fight back grateful tears and whisper my thanks.

Abigail, dressed in rich purple and belted with gold, approaches. Her transformation from the grizzled hawker always amazes me. This night she is her loveliest. "Dear little friend." She holds me. "My dear *daughter.*"

"Abigail, thank you for your kindness to me.

Thank you for all you do for Palestine." Once more we embrace, then leave to join the many who are gathered in the great hall.

Garlands of blossoms abound. Incense perfumes the cave's cool air. All torches are lit. From somewhere I hear a song played upon the instrument of ten strings.

Then everything fades into nothingness. Joel nears. His outer garment, of finely woven linen, is edged in blue fringe. A girdle embroidered in vibrant colors hugs his waist. Golden chains hang from his neck. My beloved's muscled arms are burnished in the firelight, while his raven hair glistens.

Joel's hands enfold my own. His dark eyes claim me. His love completes me. My bridegroom! Is there any person more worthy of my love? Is there another who loves me so well?

The ceremony is brief, the celebrating long, joyous, loud. Before we leave the cave and flee the congratulatory cheers, we cover our wedding finery with cloaks.

Arm in arm we amble by the shore, listening to the sea utter the song of our ecstasy. We pass through the hushed city.

"Joel? Won't the people of Caesarea wonder how you happened to obtain a bride?"

"Indeed, they will! But they already know that I never share a thing of my private life. They'll just have to conclude that I found you somewhere in my travels."

Caesarea sleeps, unknowing that Joel leads his bride through her empty streets. And oh, foolish Rome! You, too, doze. Someday, perhaps in this very city, my husband and other brave men of Palestine will openly challenge your dominion.

How strange. Joel leads us to the outskirts of the city and toward the shore. A large house—or is it a palace? rises before us. We stop at the door. Joel knocks two hard strikes, followed by three lesser raps. A man, obviously a servant, answers. He knowingly smiles at Joel, then, amidst many bows, leaves.

Brass lampstands provide light for every corner of this grand room. Opulent furniture and potted plants tastefully decorate the area. The spotless floor is of rich mosaics.

"Where are we, Joel?" I fear arrest.

Joel laughs, hugs me, and explains, "We are home."

The thought is an impossible one. "But Abigail said you'd probably fold up your tent and move in with us."

"And you believed her?"

I stare in disbelief. Never have I seen such luxury. Overwhelmed, I conclude, "You must be an excellent physician."

"The procurator gave me this house when I helped his chief mare to foal. Then too, the rich of this city pay me handsomely for tending their ills.

"Much of my wealth goes to our cause, of course. But Abigail insists that I entertain wealthy and important Romans. I do this to ward off any suspicions." He gathers me in his arms. "Whatever I own, Marah, is now also yours."

Joel guides me to a balcony overlooking the Great Sea. Baskets of pink flowers hang from the high arches. Joel again embraces me. For a long moment we savor our love.

Beyond another archway I spy a most beautiful room. Although it is veiled by a sheer curtain, a trio of lamps burning within the area bring it into clear view. Centered in the room lies a rose damask bed. Graceful urns of fresh blossoms are positioned in the corners. A breeze from the sea stirs the bedroom curtains, bidding us to come.

How far away are the green slopes . . . the rough robes of the goatherd . . . the bleatings . . . the dreariness.

And yet. . . .

SEVENTEEN

Rome may rule the world, but Tryphosa definitely governs our household. This wizened, opinionated woman supposedly serves as cook. I find, however, that she is overseer, taskmaster, steward, and watchdog.

In the beginning days of our marriage I complained to my husband, "That woman resents any order I give her!"

"Tryphosa resents any order from anyone," he had said. "But this house depends on her. Besides, she makes a delectable stew."

During these almost three years as Joel's wife, I, too, have fallen captive to Tryphosa. I am careful not to leave clutter or footprints. If I do manage to win her approval in some matter, my spirit soars. Tryphosa is gifted in tyranny.

This day she directs me to a closet. "Marah,

pregnant women sometimes throw up for a spell," she brusquely divulges this not-so-secret information. "Use this basin. I don't want a mess to clean up." I am with child and remember to use the appointed basin when necessary.

Long ago, following the beating I received when Sandalmaker and I moved trumpets, Joel questioned the wisdom of my Mareshah disguise. "That villain saw her headpiece fall and her hair loosen. If even one person suspects," he had argued, "our whole system is endangered." I recall the tender way he had regarded me. Now that I am with his child, he absolutely refuses to allow any possibility of peril to come to me. And so I aid the cause by entertaining Roman elite.

Tonight we host the newly appointed centurion, Cornelius. He is an elegant man. I find it hard to believe that he supports Rome with such enthusiasm. I wish he were one of us.

Tryphosa receives our tall visitor. Unimpressed by his status or stature, she commands, "Shake off that dirt before you walk on my clean floor!"

Joel rushes to rescue Cornelius lest Tryphosa inflict further insult.

"Welcome, my friend," greets Joel, slapping the Roman's back. "Please come in and be comfortable." To Tryphosa he suggests, "We need refreshments for our guest." She scowls briefly at the centurion, then hustles off to see to her task.

Cornelius sighs and sinks back into a large pillow. "What a captain she'd make." We laugh, picturing this small lady brandishing a sword and leading her troops.

"Joel, look at your wife. She is prettier than ever." Then, in mock dismay, Cornelius wrings his hands. "Joel, if only Rome would order you to improve your appearance."

My husband pretends to hurl a weapon. Cornelius clutches his shin in feigned pain. Tryphosa, bearing a tray filled with bread and cheese, shoots a threatening look toward both men. By their foolishness not one thing had better be upset or broken. Satisfied that her silent warning has been understood, she marches out for the remainder of our repast.

For several minutes we chat about the problems facing centurions and physicians. Cornelius dusts the bread crumbs from his lap onto the floor. Remembering Tryphosa, he hurries to sweep them up into his hand and drops the bits back onto the tray.

"Joel and Marah, I need a favor from you. There is a poor family in the Jewish sector." Joel and I exchange glances. There are many poor among the Jews. "It is the family of Ezra. His sight is nearly gone. And he has a large family. They are nearly destitute."

I glance about our luxurious room and am overcome with guilt.

"How may we help?" asks Joel.

"They are in need of everything . . . food, clothes, blankets . . . whatever you can spare. I've given some things, but it isn't enough."

Eavesdropping as usual, Tryphosa interrupts, "I'll prepare a food basket."

"Thank you," says Joel, dismissing her. "Of course we'll provide the items and a purse of coins." I am grateful for my husband's generosity.

Joel considers Cornelius momentarily. "Tell me, my friend, what is your interest in these poor? I know this isn't the first time you've aided some impoverished Jew."

Cornelius laughingly explains, "Well, I'm certainly not trying to recruit soldiers for Caesar from that crowd!" He swallows several grapes. "My patrol took me through the Jewish sector. I pitied the very poor and sometimes brought food. Other times I offered clothes my children had outgrown. After some time I began to observe that these destitute people owned something quite remarkable. They enjoyed a God unlike any of the gods I knew.

"They told me stories of this mighty God. They sang of his splendor and righteousness. And more. This God forgave them, freely and totally.

"I had never heard of such a deity in all my life. The gods of Rome offer no compassion.

"Before long I knew it wasn't just my concern for their poverty which drew me again and again to these Jews. I wanted to know this wondrous Lord God."

His eyes glisten and his voice is merry. "I pray to him daily. I believe, when Messiah comes, I shall know him even more fully."

Joel softly comments, "Cornelius, our Lord is marvelous indeed. I am happy that you know him."

Later, after our guest has left, Joel rubs his

head and comments, "Perhaps we'd do better to convert Rome."

"What will you name your baby?" asks Abigail.

Her hair is now almost as white as Sweeper's. In the cave's torchlight it shines like polished silver. "We've selected two names. If we have a son, we'll call him Abner. Joel sorely misses the old man and wishes to honor his memory. But if our child is a girl," I pause and gently tap my middle, "if we have a daughter we'll name her after our dear friend, Abigail."

She gasps, claps her hands, and squeezes me. I do believe she is pleased.

The meeting at the cave is ended. The latest trick we played on Rome was to intoxicate the parade horses. How foolish, how utterly foolish those riders looked, trying to guide their drunken mounts. Reviewing the scene, we laugh until we can laugh no more.

As always, in conclusion, we circle the table, join arms, and hear Abigail's familiar words encouraging our efforts and invoking the blessings of God.

Jealously I watch as group after group is dismissed. I am very tired tonight and desirous to be on my way. Sweeper and Carpenter, standing under the beamed archway, call Joel and me over to share a few private words. I lean against a wooden support and wait. Abigail and the remaining few linger at the table enjoying a story about Tiberias.

A jolt suddenly shakes the ground. Immediately there follows a deep rumble. The cave heaves and sways.

"Earthquake!" someone yells.

Loosened dirt from above hammers my head. A torch is thrown from its anchor. Our friends jump away from the table, but the undulating floor hinders their steps. Shouts of warning and alarm are dwarfed by the deafening roar of falling earth. I throw my hands over my face and scream until the dust chokes my cries.

The horror lasts for an instant, for an eternity. Then it ends. I open my eyes. All is dark save a lone torch. Implausibly, it yet burns.

"Marah?" I hear his voice, "Marah?"

"Joel," I cough and call again.

My husband's arms, his solid arms, are about me, stilling my trembling. "Are you all right?" he pleads. I dismiss the slight hurts. "I think so, and you?"

Grateful to be alive and together, we cling to one another for a long moment.

"The others! We must find the others!" Joel climbs over the rubble to the torch, unhooking it from its fastening. It is then we realize there are additional lights above us. Through the haze of settling dust we discern the stars, unshaken and undisturbed.

Much of the cave has collapsed. Joel swings the light about. Destruction is everywhere. Only the area supported by the strong rafters remains unfallen.

The beams, Carpenter's carefully set beams, saved us!

"Marah, Sweeper, and Carpenter were with

us when the earthquake struck. They must be nearby."

We hear a cough. "There, over there!" A gray ghost of a person emerges from the ruins Joel indicated. "Carpenter?"

"I'm all right," he says, brushing the dirt from his garments. Then he coughs and repeats, "I'm all right." In the flickering light of the single torch I see bleeding from his arm, but judge it not a serious wound.

From somewhere comes a moan. We step over debris and listen. There it is again. The three of us crawl over the wreckage to its source. The bent form of Sweeper sobs over a half-buried body. Joel lowers the light and he, too, weeps aloud.

Abigail is dead. Killed in the very grotto which gave her such protection. Our grief staggers us.

"We tried to reach each other," groans Sweeper, his white hair darkened by dirt and dust. "A few steps either way and we'd both be alive or both finished." Sweeper lies over the body and gives vent to his anguish.

The next moments are spun of nightmarish threads. Threatening tremors continue. We search and call and dig among the waste. At last we conclude that all have perished. Only we four survive the cave's collapse.

The exit tunnel is blocked. The only way out is up. We pile the rubble to provide steps to the surface. Before we attempt the ascent we lock arms and for the last time Joel haltingly speaks the benediction we so recently heard from Abigail.

Finished with the arduous climb, we drop to the cool earth. Our rest is brief. The earthquake also struck the city. We see the distant fires and hear the faint shouts.

Joel calls us to focus on our predicament. "Our cave is destroyed. There are many who left before the quake hit. Undoubtedly they will regroup and the cause will soon trouble Rome once more. But when this devastation is discovered and searched, my safety will be in jeopardy. There are items and writings that can tie these activities to me. Marah and I must leave Caesarea."

"Now?" I whimper. "Tonight?"

"Time is our ally if we leave right away."

I caution, "Already I am so weary that even a brief walk seems impossible. Joel, I don't know how well I can travel."

Carpenter's husky voice offers hope, "You know I have a small fishing boat. It wasn't built for the open sea, but if you sail near land it should serve you well. Marah could rest in it as you travel."

Joel mulls over our plight. "The boat is our best choice. Thank you, friend."

Sweeper sighs, "Let me go with you. There is nothing here for me anymore." A massive sob shakes him.

Carpenter leads us to his boat's mooring place. "I have family in the city. I must go now and see how they fare." He explains to Joel and Sweeper how to handle the craft. It is time to bid our friend farewell. Joel grasps Carpenter's shoulders, "Take charge of our cause. God be with you. Perhaps we shall meet again in the free Palestine."

Joel tenderly lifts me into the vessel. Silently we three drift from land. The sail won't be raised until light. Joel removes his cloak and bundles it about me. "Rest now."

The waves are moderate. I watch through sleepy eyes as the men row us away from Caesarea. Fires, caused by the earthquake, burn. As we move along the water the flames become but tiny sparks. I wonder if we ever will see this beautiful city again.

Sweeper's white hair catches the starlight.

"Were you and Abigail more than friends?" In this moment my question is not impertinent.

He maintains the rhythm of his strokes, "We were."

Memories and grief wrap us in a silent melancholy. Sweeper blows his nose over the black sea and informs, "If morning brings a good wind we will dock at Tyre. A shipper there is one of us. We'll take on supplies and sail north to Seleucia."

"Seleucia! Who there can help us?" I weep.

Sweeper consoles, "Abigail knew people all over. Often she mentioned to me her friends in Seleucia. We will find them and they will help us."

It is all too much. I cry uncontrollably, "Oh, Joel, what of our home? What's to become of us?"

Joel strokes my hair. "Our home, Marah, is us. And we are safe."

In the palled light of this predawn I look into

my husband's perfect face. I love him so, but my fear screams at me. "Help me to not be afraid."

"My love," he soothes, "God is with us."

I look about . . . the Great Sea . . . our frail boat. "Is he, Joel, is he way out here where we drift unseen?"

Joel reaches for my hand. "Remember our Psalms? There is one written for just such an occasion as this. It speaks of God's nearness. I memorized it while still a boy."

I lean against Joel and wait for the words.

Where can I go from your Spirit?
Where can I flee from your presence?
If I go up to the heavens, you are there;
if I make my bed in the depths, you are there.
If I rise on the wings of the dawn,
if I settle on the far side of the sea,
even there your hand will guide me,
your right hand will hold me fast.

Far side of the sea . . . even there! Joel drops his hand onto mine, then lifts my chin. He prays, "Lord God, you hold the seas as we would hold a bird. Please also hold my Marah. If our lives should be lost, please spare and protect her."

In the solace of his prayer I find comfort. The sun eases through the horizon. The men raise the sail and catch the breezes that cool the shore. Effortlessly we move northward.

It is yet early morning when the air is charged with fierce gusts. Clouds lower, hiding the sun. Land, too, vanishes as fog and rains mingle. The salt spray envelopes us. It becomes a struggle for

Joel and Sweeper to keep our boat afloat on these disturbed waters. Before they can lower the sail, furious winds shred the canvas. We are without course, without direction. We are but a toy tossed about by the whims of this terrible storm.

"Have you any idea how long this might last?" shouts Joel.

Sweeper pushes wet strands of hair away from his eyes. "Sailors say that the sea is given to sudden fits, some lasting hours, some even days."

Giant swells raise and drop our craft into watery valleys, again and again. With my hands I try to scoop out the flood filling the boat. It is useless. Suddenly we are thrust into a wild spin. Sweeper yells something to Joel. I can't discern his words above the tumult of the winds, but I do hear the sickening screech of boards being torn from the bow. Sweeper grabs for the boat's edge as a wall of gray water strikes, sucking him overboard. Aghast, Joel and I can only watch as the deep swallows our friend. I retch.

Joel screams and gestures for me to stay low. Rains pelt us. I wail, unheard. The ravaging current jerks and pounds our broken vessel. I try to crawl to the side where Joel struggles to control our direction. An imposing wave swiftly lifts our craft only to heave us into a canyon of black. The boat explodes. Joel is beyond my reach. I thrash in the cold, churning water. Joel! Boards hurled by a cruel force crash upon my husband's head. The dark water reddens.

Joel! Joel!

Only the storm answers. The chilly brine

engulfs me. . . . *If I make my bed in the depths, you are there* . . . spinning walls of black . . . *even there* . . . *your hand*. . . . Joel! Oh, Joel! . . . *will hold me fast.*

EIGHTEEN

Darkness.
  Swirling.
    Murky shadows.
      I am adrift in a vast, bleak void.
Remnant cries evaporate into the night mists. Screaming is stilled. Yet from the distant edges of ebony circles I hear sounds. A woman's voice soothes, "There, there. You are safe. Please try to rest."

"Is the lady alive?" Another voice, tiny and far away.

A man speaks, "Her thrashing has lessened. Soon we can untie her arms."

Whom do they discuss? My head! Why this ceaseless reeling? Where are my hands? I spin end over end. *No more, oh, please, no more!* I am sick, so sick. . . .

Other hands support my head, directing the vomiting.

Images of angels and demons gyrate about me. I try to focus on these twisting forms. The figures narrow, merging into one substance . . . a flame, a lantern alone on a table.

I cough.

"Easy, dear." It is the woman again.

She props a pillow beneath my head and offers wine from a cup. My head throbs. I sip, then drink all of it.

The woman removes the emptied cup. She unfolds a large blanket, covers me, rests her hand momentarily on my cheek, then steps away.

Day and night intertwine. I cannot settle if I sleep for days, or if only moments pass between my wakings.

Upon every opening of my eyes I see the woman. Her smile and touch comfort me. She is pleasant to look upon and does her tasks with a quiet grace.

At times a child hovers near my bed. She is too little to wear such anxiety upon her face.

A third person, a stout man, appears periodically in the far corner. Now he paces and scratches his mottled beard. "Where do you think she is from?"

The woman shakes her head. "The poor thing, her face is so swollen and discolored it is impossible to guess her nationality."

I try to speak but find myself whirling into black nothingness. I struggle, but cannot escape.

Consciousness progressively shoves aside the bands of sleep. Dizziness and pain have eased. I rub the crusts from my eyes. The daylight reveals that I am in a large room. It is neat and comfortably furnished. The woman is seated and stitching. My movings catch her attention. She drops the sewing and is at my bedside. She lifts my hand.

"You have been through a great deal."

I close my eyes and try to recall. No memories come, only tears.

"Go right ahead and cry. God gave us tears to wash away our hurts."

I feel my other hand being gathered into a small grasp. I turn and meet a large pair of somber brown eyes.

"Are you alive?" inquires a wisp of a child.

I nod my affirmation.

"Who are you?" she demands.

Again nothing comes.

The little girl drops my hand. "My name is Elisabeth. I am almost four years old." She squints her eyes at me, shrugs her shoulders, and leaves.

The woman smiles after the child, then pulls a stool to my side.

"My name is Tabitha. You are in Joppa. This is my home."

"How . . .?" I am too weak to complete my question.

"How did you get here? Well, I can tell you what I know. You were in a shipwreck."

A shipwreck! I vainly try to remember.

The woman, Tabitha, rises, goes to a cupboard, and returns with a bowl. "You need to regain strength. Here, drink a little of this broth."

She raises my head, then slowly pours the beverage into my mouth. Satisfied that I am on my way to restored health, she continues, "You were barely alive when Caleb found you floating on that island of lumber almost a week ago."

I lift my eyebrows. Tabitha laughs and pats her knee. "Caleb is a fisherman . . . father of little Elisabeth. It is a fortunate thing that your clothing snagged on those boards. Surely God's hand kept you safe."

Tabitha pauses. "That's enough talk for now. You should rest."

Exhaustion simplifies my obedience.

"Is she still alive?" It must be the child again.

"Yes, dear, but I believe she is sleeping."

"I picked her some flowers."

"Well, bless you, Elisabeth. When the lady wakes up I'm sure she will be cheered by your gift."

"Let's wake her up!"

"No, she needs to rest."

I open my eyes. Tabitha frowns at the little girl. Undaunted, Elisabeth spreads her bouquet across my feet.

"Do you know your name yet, lady?"

I shake my head.

"I could give you a name if you want me to." She stands with her hands on her hips. "I like the name Hannah. We could call you that." I smile my consent.

Now that I have a name I decide to try sitting up. But my head begins to float away. I pitch over. Tabitha catches me. "Regaining lost strength takes time. Don't be discouraged, dear."

I fall back upon my pillow and submit to the healing oblivion of sleep.

"How is our visitor from the sea?" calls the stout man, entering Tabitha's doorway.

"Daddy!" heralds Elisabeth as the man plucks the child from his legs and lifts her over his head. "Daddy, come and see the lady. She can open her eyes and even say some words." As they near my cot Elisabeth places her tiny hand on the man's whiskered mouth. "She doesn't know who she is, so don't ask her." Brightening, she adds, "But we call her Hannah."

He gently puts Elisabeth down and stands smiling above me. "Hello, Hannah." His voice is soft. "I'm happy to see you awake. I am Caleb."

I extend a hand to my rescuer and murmur, "Thank you . . . Caleb."

Tabitha enters the room. She boasts of my progress, then suggests that I be allowed to rest. I close my eyes and listen to their conversation.

"The port of Joppa is full of talk about that earthquake that recently shook Caesarea."

"What have you learned?" asks Tabitha.

"The news is sad. Many were killed outright. Many others were injured. Homes flattened in moments." Caleb's voice lowers. "The major reports concern a cave near the city. It collapsed during the earthquake, burying several people."

These words disturb me, yet I am fascinated with the telling. I strain to catch every word.

Caleb continues with his information. "That

cave was a secret meeting place for a scattering of patriots." Suddenly he starts to laugh, "Imagine, a band of rebels operating beneath the procurator's own city! I'll bet Rome was livid with the news!" He roars now. I open my eyes.

"Caleb! Not so loud," admonishes Tabitha nodding toward me.

He half smiles, first at Tabitha, then at me. "Sorry." In a sober tone he addresses the woman: "Word is that a Jew, a doctor, led the dissenters. His body wasn't among those found in the rubble. The authorities are searching for him. Poor man, better stay hidden. Rome will kill him for sure!"

I close my eyes and pray for the vanished doctor.

"Hannah?" The call repeats, "Hannah?"

I blink and see a tiny face staring into mine. "You've been sleeping a long time," she accuses.

"Elisabeth! I told you to let the lady sleep." Tabitha pulls the little girl away from my bedside and inspects my face.

"How are you feeling, dear?"

"Better." My words come easier now. I stretch and start to sit. To my shock I discover that I am hemorrhaging. Tabitha sees my distress.

"Oh, look, Elisabeth," she points, "that kitten is back and by the tree."

Exit Elisabeth.

Tabitha gathers a few rags from a basket near my bed and hands me the wad.

"Something is wrong!" I lament.

Her face confirms my statement, but she insists, "You are fine. In a few more days you'll be strong again."

Yet in Tabitha's soft eyes I see sorrow, my sorrow.

Tugging at her sleeve, I plead, "Tell me."

She sighs and hesitates, then says, "You miscarried only hours after your arrival." I stare at the beams of the ceiling.

"Miscarried?"

"The midwife said you were about four months into your term. Hannah, you are a healthy woman, strong even to have survived all you have. Be grateful."

I don't move. I think about this lost baby. Who was the father? Who am I?

"Tabitha, are you telling me everything? Did the midwife say more?"

The woman's eyes fill with tears. "Yes. She said you'd probably not have more children."

My past is lost to me and now my future too. Tabitha's arms surround me. I perceive we share a woe that rests heavily upon a woman. So much is hidden from me, so much is gone. But this I own; I have the caring of a kind friend.

We are interrupted by the squeals of a tiny captor proclaiming her victory. The kitten has been apprehended. "Look! Look!" Elisabeth holds a fluff of gray under her chin. Excitedly she hobbles to my bed.

Hobbles! Oh no, the child has a twisted foot!

The kitten is dropped by my ear. "Listen to her purr, Hannah. She's glad you are here." The animal licks my cheek. Elisabeth throws back her head and laughs just like . . . just like who?

154

NINETEEN

Daily my injuries abate and strength increases. Still I have no recollection of my identity or past.

"Tabitha, during the times I was delirious, did I call out a name or speak of anyone? Do you know anything about my past at all?"

The woman slowly unwinds the thread from the long spool. "No, no I can't think of a thing that might hint of your past. I can tell you, though, that your clothes, shredded as they were, had been costly." She bites the thread at the desired length. Perhaps you were the wife of a merchant, joining him on a buying trip."

"Were?"

"No one else survived that shipwreck, dear. Caleb saw nothing save the boards carrying you. He even asked the other fishermen if they'd come across any evidence of the tragedy. Sometimes, Hannah, the sea hammers a boat and not even a splinter is found."

I am bereft. Of certainty I must be a recent widow, yet no face comes whereupon I may place my grief.

Tabitha redirects our conversation. Raising the new coat she is making, she proposes, "Would you like to try stitching a seam?"

The garment merges obediently in my hands. Clearly I've sewn before. Where? Oh, where? I tug at the thread and break it too soon. "Tabitha, I can't recall a thing!"

"Then we will just be content that you are alive and recovering so speedily. See here, I've a surprise for you."

She rummages momentarily in a large basket of fabric, then brings forth material rivaling the gold of her garden flowers. "Your depressions must cease, dear. How about it if we make you a dress so pretty that your spirit will have to laugh?"

Clothed in the soft folds of my new outfit and warmed by the morning sun, I happily join Tabitha and Elisabeth on this major outing.

"You can't manage much longer with my cast-off shoes. Simon is a fine tanner. He will fix you up, in no time, with sandals."

Our walk takes us seaward. "Does this Simon live near the beach?"

"That he does." Tabitha laughs under her breath. "Soon you'll understand why it is a blessing for him to be so located."

Little Elisabeth scurries ahead of us in chase of a butterfly. "She moves right well in spite of her handicap," comments Tabitha. "Caleb is my kinsman. His wife died over a year ago while giving birth to a stillborn son. Since then, I've prepared supper for Caleb and the child. When he fishes, Elisabeth stays with me. I've tried to be a comfort to them. Poor man mourned so for his wife. It's only lately that he's been himself." Tabitha sighs and gazes heavenward. Her words seem more directed there than to me. "Caleb should marry and have a regular home."

Elisabeth returns with the captured butterfly. "Look," she demands, opening her hands. I turn away, not wanting to see this lovely winged creature crumpled. "Hannah, look!" I force myself to obey. Unharmed and thoroughly beautiful, the butterfly rests in her small palm.

"He didn't know who he was either, so I told him that it didn't matter. He was just as pretty as if he did." Her brown eyes underscore the tender point. With a quick puff she blows the unremembering butterfly on his way. Her hand slips into mine and we walk in amiable understanding.

A harsh gust brings an odor so pungent I almost gag. Protectively pinching my nostrils, I beg, "What is that?" Elisabeth covers her mouth to hide her giggles. Tabitha explains the stench. "We are near the tanner's. Usually we're not greeted quite this markedly. The sea breezes almost always dissipate those awful smells." Now I understand the reason for his beach location. The little girl tugs at my hand, "Hurry. Simon's a nice man."

Simon *is* a nice man. Right off, I like this affable tanner. His arms are grand with muscles earned by his profession.

"So this is the lady Caleb pulled from the sea! I would gladly take up fishing if I thought I might make such a catch." He roars over his joke. A halo of red fuzz covers all of Simon—all, that is, save his bald head. And that surface shines like the sea beneath the sun.

In no time he presents me a pair of newly fashioned sandals. Tabitha's offer of payment is soundly rejected. "The sea stole her shoes." He waves toward the mass of blue. "Since I own this edge of the water it is only fair that I make Hannah new sandals."

The argument is ended.

On the way home Tabitha asks if I am up to a brief visit to the marketplace. Buoyed by excitement, I tell her yes.

The tranquility of the sea has no influence here. Buyers shove themselves to the booth of choice. Little courtesy is given to the child with a twisted foot. I try to shield her from the crowd.

Tabitha wants cheese. Several young goats stand tethered near the cheese stall. Elisabeth limps to the animals to offer her gift of fresh weeds. She chortles as they nibble at her fingers. One goat lowers his head. Suddenly I am engulfed in a strange terror. I scream a warning and snatch the surprised Elisabeth into a violent embrace. She begins to cry. Tabitha rushes to us. "Hannah, what is it?" I can't answer, I can only cling to the sobbing child.

The goats bleat their confusion. People gape at us. The shopkeeper worries aloud that I might have a demon. Tabitha does her best to calm all of us. At last my fright subsides and the crowds go their way. As Tabitha pays for the cheese, the shopkeeper watches my every move. It isn't good for business to have a woman go insane so near his wares.

"Are you all right, Hannah?"

"Yes, Elisabeth, I'm fine now."

Relieved, the child runs ahead of us to check on mysteries hidden from adult eyes.

"Tabitha, I have no explanation for what happened. I saw the goat step toward Elisabeth and panic overwhelmed me."

"There must be a reason for your fear. We need to understand that. For now we'll be satisfied with your healing and present blessings."

The little girl scurrying before us must head that list of blessings. Every day she brings new delight to my life. Her sweet ways truly aid my recovery. Her laughter is forerunner of sunshine and birdsong. She must sense my thoughts, for she turns and grins at me. One small hand straightens her dress while the other pushes an auburn lock away from her face. Elisabeth's hair typifies her person, soft, untamed, and bouncing in every direction at once. I pity the mother who can no longer enjoy the beauty of this little girl, this brave little girl who never complains about her twisted foot.

Sewing must have been important in my life, for I discover I am very able to bring garments into being.

"Hannah, I do thank God for your skill. Now we can provide coats for people who otherwise would be cold."

I fold the garment I have just completed. Tabitha is a landowner, so I know she has the means. However, I'm curious. "Why do you feel so duty-bound, Tabitha, to clothe every vagrant and waif in Joppa?"

Tabitha smiles and her eyes crinkle about the corners. "Not duty-bound, not duty-bound at all. God has been so generous to me. My late husband left a great deal of wealth. I only wish to share my bounty." She inspects the robe she has been stitching. "Hannah, God is good. I want others to rejoice in his goodness."

An unexpected anger from some inner depth rises to challenge her words. "Good? Is it goodness that hides my yesterdays from me? See my arm, shall we count the scars? And what about the very people you sew for? Is it a benevolent God who from the warmth of his heavens watches their shivering? Tell me, how is it that a God who is good can stand by and watch helmeted soldiers enslave nations? And why . . . why the twisted foot of an innocent child?"

How can I be so rude to this gracious woman? Immediately I apologize.

Tabitha reaches for my hand. "That's all right. I wish that you and I could stop all suffering. But don't scold the questionings of your mind. Doubt is the cornerstone of faith."

She rises and pours two goblets of wine. "We need to rest our eyes a spell.

"You know, Hannah, if I'd never seen the brilliance of day, I would not think to light a lamp to oppose night's darkness. If God were not ab-solutely good, the idea of evil would have no

160

basis for distressing you. But he is good and you see evil as foe to that good. My dear, I am only a simple woman, tainted by a sinful nature, yet I want to ease all the discomforts I can. Just think how God, perfect in his love, must anguish over all that hurts us."

Could that be so? Does God feel my woes?

Do I view the wrongs of life against the backdrop of God's goodness?

Is the darkness of my soul seen because of the Lord who is light?

TWENTY

Cool weather will soon be upon us. Half-completed coats bestow little warmth. Tabitha and I accelerate our sewing efforts. Elisabeth, wanting to be of service, sprawls upon the floor and rolls threads about a stick.

"Hannah," she looks up from her windings, "did you know that God is going to lose his memory too?"

"No, I didn't know that."

"Well, he is. Tabitha told me so."

I glance at my friend. She merely lifts her eyebrows. "And how," I ask, "does she know that?" Tabitha is knowledgeable, but this?

"A long time ago there was a prophet named Jeremiah. He told people what God wanted said. Right Tabitha?"

"That is so, Elisabeth."

"Well, God told him that someday he would make a new covenant with us. When that happens," her earnest eyes widen, "God says he will remember our sins no more."

"My!" How else can I respond?

She stands and brushes the lint from her clothes. "You will be really happy then. Maybe God will forget my sins, *but* I'll always know what I've done." The little girl waves her arms. "Oh, Hannah, do you realize that neither you nor God will ever recall a single bad thing about you?"

It is late afternoon when Tabitha asks the child and me to harvest a few figs. I do the picking while Elisabeth holds the basket aloft. "Drop the fruit gently. Daddy doesn't like mushy figs."

My thoughts twirl about in my mind. I have done this task before.

"Hannah, can you reach those uppermost figs?"

Those words! I've heard this very request before. Yes, I see the woman, round, red, and out of breath. Anna! Oh, where do I know her from? My heart skips with excitement. Even though answers elude me, this is the first clear image to come from my past.

"Can you, Hannah?" Elisabeth brings me to the moment. I pick the higher figs.

Having filled the basket, I rest in the tree's shade. Elisabeth, not in the least tired, drags a stick about the soft ground. "See, I made a bird!" Sure enough, she has outlined a bird in flight. This beautiful child, so hindered in her steps, soars in the simple drawing.

She drops to my side. "Elisabeth, does it ever bother you that your foot is twisted?" I touch the thick, unsightly callus on the outside of her small foot. She pulls her skirt past her knees to study both feet. "It isn't as pretty as my other foot, is it? But see, it is only a little bent." She grins and says, "It is better than if I didn't have a foot at all." Pushing her skirt down, she peers up into my face.

"Does it bother *you?*"

I lift her into my arms and know of a certainty, "No, my darling Elisabeth. No, no, no." As she settles into my embrace I recall holding another child, a little boy who laughed at the sun and ran unhindered.

"Hannah, why are your eyes all wet?"

Tabitha stands hesitating in the doorway. "Are you certain that you feel up to watching over Elisabeth for a month?"

I gently shove my friend and her basket of food and clothing out the door. "Go, be with Mary. Goodness knows, with new twin boys she will be overjoyed to have your help."

"And you don't mind feeding Caleb? You know he can't cook a thing."

"Tabitha, go! I can manage both Caleb and Elisabeth and your house as well. You all have done so much for me. It's now my turn to be of service."

She starts to speak, laughs, then announces, "I'll have a grand time with two babies to play with."

I bring Elisabeth again to the fig tree, hoping to shake out a few more memories. The little girl finds a stick and again becomes the artist of the soft dirt.

Impulsively I turn into teacher. I have no recollection of my own schooling, I only know that I am educated.

"Did you know that words can be drawn?"

"How?"

I clear her artwork with a swatch of leaves. Using her stick, I write her name. "There. That says *Elisabeth.*"

She frowns. "It doesn't look like me at all."

"Words don't have to look like what they say." I write my name, and Tabitha's, and Caleb's. It isn't until I write *bird* that she understands the meaning of the written word.

Elisabeth hungers for more instruction. I delight in sharing knowledge with her. As I do, shadowy pieces of my own education cross my thoughts. My teacher's face comes to mind. Strangely, my heart lovingly responds to the image. Could my teacher have been my father? I am as one examining a mound of broken pottery, attempting to reconstruct some unknown item. I long for the potsherd to take form.

Caleb stretches out upon Tabitha's best cushion and rubs his shoulder. "Great catches of fish are desirable, but not without penalty." He is a pleasant man, patient and thoughtful. "The child talks about you all the time. Claims you are the world's best teacher."

"Elisabeth is an eager student."

"You are good with the child. I haven't seen her this happy since . . . well, for a long time." He stretches and again massages his shoulder.

165

As I turn to bring him wine there comes a rapid knocking at the door. The visitor is an angular woman, younger than Tabitha, and almost pretty. Behind her stands a pouty child of about ten.

"I heard that Tabitha is gone for a few weeks," she begins. Her voice is high pitched and authoritative. "I came to invite Caleb for a supper. I know you've been injured and probably aren't able to do much for the man."

Elisabeth is at my side and scowls at the girl before her. The visiting girl sticks out her tongue. Elisabeth ignores the girl and greets the woman with cool politeness, "Hello, Bashemath."

"Sweet little Elisabeth," gushes the woman, "have you been eating well?" Elisabeth backs away from the outstretched arms.

Remembering Tabitha's insistence that her home is open to all, I invite these people to come in. Bashemath heads straight for Caleb. "Oh, Caleb. Sweet little Elisabeth is so pale. You must let me take her home for a few days, poor little crippled thing."

Caleb pats Elisabeth's head. "Hannah here is providing fine care for the child. Would you like to sit down?"

The woman nervously titters and finds a chair near Caleb. We are introduced. Elisabeth, mindful of her manners, invites the girl, Rachel, outside to play. Rachel stares at Elisabeth's twisted foot, turns to her mother, and asks, "Do I have to?"

After the children leave, Bashemath again states her business. She definitely wants Caleb to join her in a very soon repast. To gild the bidding, she insists that "sweet little Elisabeth" must also come. I notice the lack of my inclusion. Rubbing her hands together, she smiles fetchingly at Caleb, "Well?"

I don't like this woman.

"Your invitation is kind, Bashemath. But Hannah is doing quite well in filling in for Tabitha. Thank you anyway."

I know she must be disappointed, but the smile of a moment ago remains fixed.

"Of course, Caleb, whatever you say."

She rises, glances unappreciatively toward me, and moves to the door.

Sweet little Elisabeth calls the farewell after our visitors.

Coming back into the house, she mumbles, "That Rachel is mean. She said I walk funny and that my foot is ugly. I should've hit her."

Caleb chuckles. "Hannah, you've just met the widow Bashemath and her daughter. Her husband fell from a building about eight years ago. Some folks think he jumped. Since then she has been on a search for a replacement. Bashemath owns land, so it isn't a provider she needs. She frankly wants a man. Every widower in Joppa has been invited for supper. My own wife had been dead but a few days when she started after me. And she hasn't let up the chase."

Elisabeth grabs her throat. "You won't marry her, will you?"

Caleb breaks into laughter. "No, not even if we have to cook our own meals."

It is late when Caleb carries his drowsy daughter back to their home.

"Has any of your memory returned?" Caleb reaches for his third portion of broiled fish. "She doesn't need to remember," defends Elisabeth. "We like Hannah just fine as she is."

"We do indeed," agrees Caleb.

Following supper, Elisabeth perches upon her father's lap. As I clear away the mounds of fish skeletons, the little girl chatters non-stop.

Finished with the small chores, I recline upon a pile of cushions and join in their pleasantries.

"I heard a song today from another fisherman." Caleb's warm voice chants a tale of a greedy fish who gobbled a whole net of fishes, fifteen boats, and finally his own tail. Elisabeth yawns, and with a smile upon her face, falls asleep.

"These evenings with you and the child," Caleb pauses, "I've enjoyed these moments."

He stands, then carries Elisabeth to Tabitha's bed. As he moves back into the circle of the lamp's golden light, I notice that he is handsome. Caleb is really quite handsome.

"Maybe what I say will upset you. Maybe you'll never want me to come again." His eyes lower and he bites at a fingernail.

What is he wishing to tell me that causes him to struggle so?

At last he looks up. "Hannah, once I had a wife. Once you knew a husband. Now we pass through each day and night alone. I think," he examines his fingernail, "I think it would be to the benefit of each of us if we were to marry."

I am flattered, frightened, and grope for words.

"I, I am in your debt, Caleb. And more, I do

like you. But I have no name, no idea, even, of who I might be. Can you honestly want a nameless woman, with an unknown past, for your wife?"

He takes my hand. "Elisabeth and I both need you. Names and yesterday's events count for little. Besides," his eyes twinkle, "someone must save me from Bashemath."

TWENTY-ONE

"God be praised!" exults Tabitha. "Surely he brought the two of you together."

As wife of Caleb I am content. I feel growing affection for this fisherman and great love for his daughter. His house has been womanless too long. In the midst of sweeping and scrubbing, Tabitha and I agree that I came along none too soon.

Caleb accepts the new regime. Except for his wall. Both Tabitha and I are under definite orders not to even touch it. This wall, sorely in need of whitewashing, serves as display for his finds from the sea. A discarded fishnet holds dried sea creatures. Also hanging about the wall are shells, boards from shipwrecks, an old oar once belonging to a foreign galley, and things interesting only to fishermen.

As I dust near it, Caleb suddenly appears. Swooping me off the floor, he studies his wall.

"Let's see, yes, this would be the spot to hang you, my latest and favorite souvenir, from the sea." I pound his back and threaten to put holes in his boat if he doesn't put me down at once.

Elisabeth delights in our joking and adds her own humor. "Maybe you were swallowed by the same whale Jonah was. But since you tasted better, the whale didn't spit you up until Daddy came by." She giggles until we, too, join her mirth.

Silver-rimmed clouds patrol the midnight sky. Cool breezes from Joppa's coast stir the air. Unable to sleep, I stand outside in our garden, wrapped in my cover.

For the past days scant scenes of my former life have skipped into my thoughts. And now, tonight, it has all come back . . . my identity, my history. Everything at once is present.

"I missed you, Hannah." It is Caleb. "Are you having trouble sleeping?"

"Caleb. . . ." I tremble, knowing that I must reveal my past to him. "Caleb, my memory . . . even tonight . . . Caleb! I remember!"

He draws me to his side. I feel his warmth. "My real name is Marah."

He kisses me. "I can just as easily call you Marah."

"Please listen, Caleb. I know my past. I know what my life was, who I am. . . ."

"Does this mean you will leave us?"

I wipe my eyes on his sleeve. "It means you may want me to go."

He tilts my face to confront his own. "The per-

171

son I married is kind, brave, and womanly. Hannah . . . Marah . . . you daily bless my life and the life of my child. If what you remember changes any of that then I won't listen to a word of it."

His kiss is as soft as the clouds floating past the moon. Caleb secures my cover about me. "Come back to bed when you have finished with the night."

For a long while I stand staring at the place where he stood. Then views of long ago parade before me. I am a young child snuggling in my father's arms. I touch his great nose. He growls and pretends to gobble my fingers. I see my mother, frail and lovely. She calls to me. I shiver and pull my cover tighter.

Laughter pervades my musings. It is Eleazor who comes, my joyful friend and dear husband. I smile with the remembering. The scene fades and I find myself wandering among goats on a green Samaritan hill. Heber busily attends the flocks with a tireless commitment. Bouncing into view is fair Aaron, my son . . . my sun. I choke back the screams as once more I relive the horror.

The night wind increases, I drop to the ground, hoping to avoid its chill. Visions of Abigail, strange hawker and elegant leader of patriots, reaches to me. By her side stands Joel. Oh, it is Joel! Every moment with him, every embrace—every joyful embrace—is reviewed and savored. I know his arms about me, I hear that last prayer for my safety . . . I clutch my shoulders and give way to convulsing sobs. *Joel! Oh, my love! Only tonight have I found you, and that very discovery snatches you from me!*

I cover my head, trying desperately to silence the ragings of the Great Sea. My mind reels with the recollections and I collapse flat upon the ground. Still, I hear the crashings of dark walls of water. My mouth remembers the salt, the bitter taste. Joel, spinning, reaches for me. I know he cries, "Marah!" Then in red swirls, he vanishes. Joel, my dearest, my husband. . . .

The horizon declares the coming of dawn. All night I have lived the memories and I am emotionally spent. I rewrap my cover and rise to my knees. The night is over. This is a new day and I am Marah. *Marah, bitter water.* I think of that long-ago sojourn of Moses and the children of Israel, of their thirst, of the undrinkable pools, of the tree.

Somewhere there must be that tree which sweetens life's bitter waters. I mean to search until it is found.

Caleb kneels beside me. With his forefinger he brushes my hair from my face. "Your eyes are swollen from too long a cry." His calloused hand smells faintly of yesterday's catch. I press it to my lips. "Are you certain you don't want to know my past?"

His free hand lifts my chin. "I am sure, my love, I am sure."

TWENTY-TWO
❧❧❧❧❧

It must be around here someplace. Coats do not vanish into nothingness. Unless, of course, the garment belongs to Elisabeth.

"Please try to think, dear. Where were you when you last wore the coat?"

Only hours remain before the evening star signals the beginning of Sabbath rest. Our laundered clothes, the prepared meals, the filled lamps, everything is in readiness for the Lord's day of rest. Now if only Elisabeth can find her coat. I worry she will chill as we walk to and from the synagogue service tonight.

"Think, Elisabeth!"

The girl's face contorts and her brow wrinkles as she peers into her very recent past. "I remember!" she shouts. "Day before yesterday, while I played in Tabitha's garden, a whole family of butterflies came for a visit. Afterward I tried to follow them, but they flew away." She scratches her head, "Where do you think butterflies go?"

The destination of butterflies is not my major concern at the moment. Sensing this, Elisabeth lowers her eyes and mumbles, "I think my coat might be with Tabitha's flowers."

"This is the third time this month you've forgotten or misplaced something. A child of nearly seven is certainly old enough to be accountable for her own coat." I follow with a lecture on responsibility, then send her to search for the lost wrap.

As she hobbles out the door I repent for being so stern. It isn't always easy to remember things. Once, I, too, was without memory. I cringe, recalling the child's kindness to me during such difficult days.

In those times, how often we would speculate over my past. Who had I been? Where had I lived? Where was I going? Caleb and Tabitha had concluded that I probably came from the Jewish sector of some distant city. At the time I had accepted their assumption as correct. Many times, following the return of my memory, I tried to tell Caleb that I was a Samaritan, but he would not listen to a word about my former life.

Caleb is a devout Jew and diligently observes the law. For his sake I embrace as much of this faith as I can. Jewish worship is similar to that I once knew in Sebaste. I recall the blessed times we had gathering for worship in the *kinshaw*. We women, although not participants in the service, were not isolated (as it is with the Jews) from the male congregation. God was praised by the whole assembly.

I muse as to where it is that God truly wishes our worship to originate—Mt. Gerizim, as we Samaritans believe, or Jerusalem, as the Jews claim? Too many questions crowd my mind. Soon the cantor will ascend the synagogue roof and blow the three loud blasts from the ram's horn. The Sabbath will begin. What I really must concern myself with is the finding of Elisabeth's coat.

"Passover in Jerusalem is the high point of our faith, Marah. I really want you to come with me this year." Caleb joins me on the bed, lying on his side to face me. "Please don't let this be a quarrel again between us."

I've exhausted my arguments . . . Elisabeth's handicap, my dislike of mobs, the costs involved —anything to dissuade my husband from his planned pilgrimage. All that is left is just to plead.

"Caleb, I can't. I'm sorry."

He pulls me to himself. His breath is warm and mildly scented of the evening wine. He whispers into my ear, "You'd like Jerusalem, especially at holy season. Jews from all over the world will be there." He kisses my nose.

Yes, Jews from everywhere, but how many Samaritans?

This is the second Jew I've been married to. But with Joel it was different. The cause became the chief expression of our faith, the cave our holy city. These Jews of Joppa are governed by their synagogues, feast days, and rituals. Much of this religious life I can live with. But Jerusalem? How can I, a Samaritan woman, bear Passover celebration there, surrounded by numberless collections of Jews? It is more than I can manage.

I ease away from my husband's embrace. Caleb leans over me. "You are crying, Marah. Why?" His tenderness only results in the full flow of tears.

I sit up in order that I may blow my nose. Caleb, too, sits and rests his hand on my knee.

"Have you been to Jerusalem before?" His voice is gentle. "Did something painful happen to you there?"

"You never cared about my past before," I sniff.

"I'm not prying, I only want to understand." He tilts his head. "There is something about the trip that bothers you that has nothing to do with Elisabeth's foot, or crowds, or expense, isn't there?"

I stare at my empty palms. "Would it help you, Marah, to talk about it?"

I hold his rough hand to my face. Usually it comforts me. How can I tell this man, this religious Jew, that his wife is from Sebaste? Further, how can I *not* tell him? Even as I grapple with the options I drop his hand and blurt my secret.

"I am a Samaritan!"

Caleb wrings his hands. Slipping from our bed,

he steps to the other side of the room. His eyes ponder the floor as though from those straw mats wisdom might magically emerge. He says nothing.

"Caleb, I'm sorry. I should have told you that night, that night when I knew."

"No, no," at last he looks at me. "I never imagined . . . when you said that I might want you to leave us . . . I, I wondered what terrible thing lay in your past." He shakes his head. "The worst I could imagine was that you had been a harlot. For that I easily pardoned you."

"I have never been such!" I snap.

"I know, Marah, I know. Please forgive me for even thinking it."

Like a cloth soaking up a spill, I begin to absorb his words. Could it be that if one is a harlot it is excusable, whereas if one is a Samaritan. . . .

"Would you have wanted me to leave if you knew I was a Samaritan?"

"No!" he shouts, than softly adds, "I don't know." Caleb paces to the room's far corner. This strong man of the sea leans against the wall for support. Prejudice, a powerful emotion, weakens the one in which it dwells.

"Marah, this partition between Jew and Samaritan is many years in the building. We are not allowed to drink out of the same cup, and I am married to a . . ." he pounds the wall with his fist. "All my life I've thought. . . . Oh, Marah, you are more to me than anything!"

He starts to leave the room, stops and gazes back at me with moist eyes. Suddenly he is at my side, wrapped in my arms. Amidst the numerous murmurings of love, Jew and Samaritan tears mingle and wash away the great dividing wall.

"Why isn't Daddy home yet?"

"Perhaps the fishing is going exceptionally well."

It is five days since Caleb left for the sea. "Wish me well, my ladies, I go to wrestle the sea for the finest fish," he had said. I try to remember his laughing face as he bid us good-bye. But I am worried.

"Elisabeth, would you like to go with me to Joppa's harbor in the morning? Perhaps the other fishermen will know something."

Always quick for adventure, she asks, "Can we leave at first light?"

The gulls are already awake and screaming their gossip. Pieces of sunshine skip across the choppy blue waters. I search the port for Caleb's boat. Not finding it, I shield my eyes from the bright sun and scan the sea.

"Hello there, Marah!" hails the crouched old man from a pile of fish nets. "Looking for Caleb?"

"Yes. Have you seen anything of him?"

The gnarled hands pick seaweed from the edge of a net. "Not since he set sail last week. Heard, though, that the seas have been rough." He shakes the net and I know our conversation is over.

"Hannah-Marah?" Elisabeth never has ceased using her name for me. "Something bad has happened to Daddy, hasn't it?"

"We don't know that."

"He is never gone this long unless he tells us first."

"We must pray, Elisabeth, and be patient."

Patience isn't easy. It is now the eighth day since Caleb left. I try to be calm around the child, but within I relive the treachery of the sea.

The evening lamps are lit when the men arrive. The old man, along with four of Caleb's fisherman friends, stands just within the doorway. By their faces I know. Caleb has wrestled the sea and lost.

"Two other ships were in that storm," begins the old man, "these men here were in those boats. They saw Caleb's fishing companion swept overboard by the winds. Terrible winds they were. Caleb dove right in after him. The sea got them both." Another friend interjects, "All the ships were damaged. It has taken days to get them back to port. Not much is left of Caleb's boat, but we brought it back."

One by one the men pat my arm and leave.

Little Elisabeth, stunned by their news, bites a cushion, trying to stifle her sobs. I pick up Caleb's daughter and cling to all I have left of him. Racing through the darkness of the night, through the darkness of our anguish, I carry the child to Tabitha's.

We need our friend.

I am like a spider hanging from her thread, without a path, dangling alone. No more shall I joy in the returning footsteps of Caleb. Never again shall I answer his love.

Grief is not a new emotion to me. However, I

see that with the passing of years, a maturing has come. I am able to care more for another than for myself. Although my sorrow is weighty, the larger ache in my heart is for the child.

Elisabeth sits for hours before Caleb's wall of sea trophies. Sometimes she weeps, sometimes her eyes vacantly wander in her pain.

I determine to return gladness to the life of this little girl. Assured that our lunch contains Elisabeth's favorite foods, I announce to her, "Come, my small one, we are going to the beach." Without comment she caresses each item on the wall, then follows me.

The Great Sea is its loveliest. Low blue waves, edged in white, spread lazily upon the sand. A soft breeze stirs the warm air. We dig holes and watch the salt water seek out the excavations and fill them. A trio of long-legged birds chase the ebbing waves, running in retreat when the sea advances to the shore.

Elisabeth's eyes sparkle for the first time in days. It is time for lunch. We spread my cloak over the sand and unpack our food. The fresh air, coupled with the long walk, enhances our appetites. I smile as Elisabeth licks her fingers clean of the fish. I am glad to see her eat heartily once more.

Without warning, Elisabeth leaps to her feet. Grabbing handfuls of pebbles, she pelts the sea. "I hate you!" she screams. "I hate you! I hate you!" As she continues her rampage, I begin to understand. This ocean is monster, murderer. I join her outrage and hurl rocks and curses at the sea, this sea of villainy.

Exhausted, we fall sobbing upon the sand. In the rolling green hills of my homeland lies no ocean to snatch away loved ones. At last I know direction. We shall move to Sebaste.

Although Jews have no dealings with Samaritans, Samaritans are accustomed to many nationalities walking the streets. A young Jewish child would not face hostilities in my city.

After weeks of waiting, the caravan at last gathers. For only a small price, Elisabeth and I may join their company. This will not only provide us safety, but the child may ride upon a cart. We will follow the road northeast to Antipatris, ultimately to arrive in Sebaste.

Sebaste. How eager I am again to walk her fair streets. Mixed with my anticipation is the clear sorrow for the good-byes that now must be said.

Tabitha stands before us. She smiles her crinkly eyed smile and opens her basket. From it she lifts two handsome coats.

Through her tears her voice remains steady. "These are for you. You can see they are the finest I've ever made. That is because every stitch carries all my love and numerous prayers."

Elisabeth wraps her arms about Tabitha's waist. "Will you always remember me?"

"Oh my, yes. Every garment I sew I'll envision on you, my little girl. And I'll be happy for such a pretty thought."

The woman and the child face each other exchanging gentle conversation. I face the not-so-gentle words within my mind. Voices echo from other times, stirring my heart, disturbing my thoughts. I hear Tabitha, *"God is good, absolutely good."* And Caleb, *"Our faith is grand for we worship the living God."* Joel too, speaks. *"God is our righteous Shepherd."* Even my parents, *"God created all things."*

Good. Living. Righteous Shepherd. Creator. If God be all these things, is he also knowable?

I see that Elisabeth still clings to Tabitha. Her voice is filled with concern. "Will we ever be together again?"

Tabitha unwinds Elisabeth's arms and brings the small hands into position for the forthcoming kisses.

"Dear Elisabeth, does not God hold each of us in the hollow of his hand?"

"I think so."

"He does. And because that is so, we are always together."

With that, Tabitha kisses each little finger.

Now it is my turn to say good-bye to this woman who restored my life. We embrace and weep. "Good-bye, Marah. I know you leave not just to escape the sea and its reminders. You are searching for something. God will be at the end of your pursuit. You will recognize him."

TWENTY-THREE

The caravan of merchants progresses slowly. Their mission is to serve as moving marketplace of the highway. If business is good we stay put for several days, otherwise we continue our trek.

I am grateful for these new coats. Sleeping beneath the open sky and upon the ground excites the soul, but offers the body no warmth. The sea winds, reaching even this far inland, add to the night chill. Long before dawn, Elisabeth wakens, complaining of the cold.

I include her in the wrap of my cape. "Surely with both of your coats and my cape you'll soon be warm." She snuggles to my side.

"Do you know anybody in Sebaste, Hannah-Marah?"

"I haven't lived there since I was a girl. Perhaps a few of my friends might still be there."

"Will I have anyone to play with?"

I worry beyond Elisabeth's social life. This

traveling has caused her to grow frail. Soon we must be settled. The child needs to sleep indoors.

Confusion is forerunner of each day. Yet somehow the caravan assembles and we again move along. The cart Elisabeth rides upon is packed with clothing and bedding of the other travelers. She is cushioned against the many bumps, nevertheless weariness is etched upon her face.

Periodically the morning sun breaks through the overcast sky. It is during one such bright moment when the distant hill becomes distinguishable. Towering above the rolling hills and green valleys is the city. My city!

"Elisabeth," I point, "there it is!"

She sits up and strains to see what I already know. "Is it Sebaste?"

"It is! See how it glistens in the sunlight."

"Are you sure it will be as pretty as Joppa?"

"Joppa is lovely indeed, but, oh, Elisabeth, wait until you see Sebaste!"

"In the sun it looks brand new."

"Much of it is new, at least new with King Herod. But Sebaste itself is quite old. Would you like me to tell you about its beginnings?"

She nods. I notice her cheeks are pink.

Resting my hand on the wagon's rail, I begin. "Nine hundred years ago there lived a skilled soldier named Omri. He became king of all of Israel. He searched the land for a very special location to build his palace. This new ruler wanted a place of beauty, a region easily defended. One day he sighted a great rise of land

and knew at once that he must own it."

"Bet it cost him a lot of money."

"Actually he got a bargain. For just two talents of silver he bought the hill from the owner, Shemer. Omri named the new stronghold Samaria."

"Then why is it called Sebaste?"

"King Herod renamed the city to please Caesar. Remember, I told you he did much rebuilding all over Palestine? Sebaste always had been beautiful, but Herod made it even more so."

"What happened to Omri?"

"He ruled for a dozen years. After he died, his son Ahab became king. He married a princess from Phoenicia, the wicked Jezebel. Sadly, their rule was cruel and introduced idol worship. This led to sorrows, and, I believe, was the beginning of the fall of Israel."

Elisabeth sighs and leans back upon the cargo. She has had enough history.

"In Sebaste there are beautiful colonnaded streets decked with flowers. It is perfect for a little girl's wanderings."

As I follow Elisabeth's cart I reach over to push the hair out of her eyes and discover the pink in her cheeks is caused by fever.

The sun is low in the western sky when we come upon the Old Inn of Sebaste. I do not recognize the manager, a youngish woman with an oldish voice. With a quick wave of her hand she answers my appeal. "If the girl is sick I don't want her staying here with the others. Her cough will have all of them complaining to me."

The inn is a large enough room to house many

guests. But it is not in this hall I wish to stay. From my girlhood I recall a small annex adjacent to the kitchen. The woman considers it. "Well, it is vacant, but it will cost you more."

The cobwebbed chamber is without furnishings—empty, save for a mouse who dashes for cover. After spreading our mats upon the dirt floor I lay the feverish Elisabeth down. I am so grateful for even this poor lodging. The many cold nights spent beneath the sky have diminished the girl's strength. Her face is flushed and her body is hot. I try to remember what Joel would advise.

"I'm sick, Hannah-Marah."

"I know, dear. But now you can rest, soon you'll be better."

After Elisabeth has fallen asleep I take inventory of our funds. The longer-than-anticipated trip has seriously depleted the purse. We cannot afford to stay in these quarters very long. I need to find work. Perhaps the inn needs someone to do the cleaning.

I sip at the broth. It is still warm. Once again I resolve to build a good life for this sweet child of Caleb's.

The manager-woman studies me. I in turn study her. She is pretty, with flawless skin. And she is coldly polite. "Have you ever served meals to travelers?"

"I can prepare and serve meals." I avoid a direct answer.

Still holding the bowl she has overly wiped, she moves closer. "Can you clean an inn, while people yet sleep, without waking them?"

"I'm sure of it."

"The pay is meager, however, you may stay in the annex room. And if the kitchen has extra food you may have the leftovers."

"Thank you. When would you like me to start?" I can be polite also.

She arches her dark eyebrows. "My name is Shua. You will be responsible to me. I am managing the inn during my brother's absence. Be here before breakfast tomorrow."

Elisabeth grins. "My bones don't stick out so much anymore."

I feel her arms. "You are right. I'm glad to see you are well again."

"Do you have to work tonight too? I don't like it when you are gone."

"Shua makes certain that I earn my pay. I think she finds a special thrill in ordering me around. Someday, if we are watchful of our coins, we may be able to escape this woman's domination."

"Marah, after you've shaken the mats, roll them tightly, and store them in the hall cupboard."

For nearly a year now I've done this task daily. Yet Shua feels she must define its accomplishment. During the months when her brother was here she relaxed a little and was almost pleasant. But now that he is off on another journey, she is back to her old ways.

I am shaking the last mat when the man approaches. Another traveler needing lodging.

188

They come with the spring winds.

"Good day," he bows, "I am newly arrived from Pamphylia. Are you the owner of this establishment?"

I stop whipping the air with the mat. "No, you'll find her inside."

He looks into my face. "Pity."

Following the day's many duties, Elisabeth and I take our usual walk to the marketplace. Upon every visit I have trouble convincing myself that so many years have passed and so much has happened since I walked these streets as a child. Buyers still challenge sellers, Rome parades her might, animals cry, children race, and everyone pushes everyone. Yet there is a missing dimension.

The grand lady of merchandising is gone. The scene will always be incomplete without Abigail.

Elisabeth is contemplating the dark purple grapes when I feel a tug at my sleeve. "Hello again." It is the man from Pamphylia. "Since you don't own the inn, am I wrong in thinking you might own this stall of fruit?"

"I don't own anything." I didn't mean to be so self-revealing.

"Nor do I," he laughs. "It is the happiest way to live."

Elisabeth returns with the grapes of her choice. "These look good, Hannah-Marah, will they be enough?"

We make our purchase and leave.

"Who was that man?"

"Just a guest at the inn."

TWENTY-FOUR

Elisabeth is a short distance beyond our doorway, scattering breakfast crumbs for the birds.

"Good morning, young lady, and who might you be?" I hear a man address my daughter. Immediately I go to the entrance and stand hidden in shadows.

"My name's Elisabeth."

"Do you live near this inn?"

"I live right here." She waves her hand toward our annex.

"Yesterday I saw you at the marketplace with a lady. Is she your mother?"

"Was she pretty?"

"Yes, very pretty with soft green eyes. Do you know her well?"

"She's my mother."

I can't make out their further conversation, but Elisabeth is humming happily as she fairly skips into the room. I have no time to ask her about the man, as I must be at work.

Shua runs an efficient business. The customer is treated fairly and is expected to return the favor. Past Shua's professional courtesy, I find a wall of unfriendliness. In spite of my best efforts, I am unable to penetrate this barricade. Shua and I are employer and employee. I wonder if she ever feels a need for anyone?

I am almost finished with my day's work when Shua calls to me. "The guest there, the Greek from Pamphylia, wants wine. Bring him a flask right away."

Shua demands politeness in all of our dealings with the travelers, so I smile sweetly and pour his wine.

The guest pats the empty place beside him and takes the flask from my hands. I sit, intending to leave momentarily.

"I know all about you, fair lady," he begins. "You are from Joppa, the widow of Caleb, the mother of Elisabeth, and 'the nicest lady in the whole world.'"

"Did my Elisabeth tell you all that?"

"For a coin the child talked without even inhaling."

He laughs and offers to share his wine. "My name is Nicanor."

I accept the flask. "Every Greek I've ever met is named Nicanor. My name is Marah. Only places are named that."

We both laugh. It has been a long while since I've entered into a merry conversation with a man. The wine is gone, as is the sun, when I go back to my room. I hope Nicanor's stay proves a lengthy one.

Nicanor's stay is prolonged. I learn he is heir of a wealthy family of shopkeepers in Perga, the major city of Pamphylia. Summers there are harsh. This spring Nicanor's physician ordered him to leave. "For the sake of your health you must move at once to a cooler climate."

"So," this Greek tells me, "I've left Pamphylia in search of health and a new life."

"What have you done with the bowl you used for the bread crumbs?"

Elisabeth sucks in a mouthful of air. "I must've left it by the tree after I fed the birds this morning. Oh, Hannah-Marah, there was the cutest little bird. . . ."

Children can be so absent-minded. I send Elisabeth after the bowl. Shua will set up a howl if anything happens to the least of the inn's dishes.

Shua even periodically checks on our poor room. Although we have transformed the place by a thorough cleaning, the addition of a small table, and now the crimson cushion I impulsively purchased, Shua maintains her watch. I can't imagine what she fears we might do.

I step to the doorway to see what is keeping the child. The scene fills me with indignation.

Two boys and an older girl play keep-away with Elisabeth's bowl. "Here, little bent-foot," taunts one boy, "do you want the dish?" As Elisabeth hobbles to him he tosses it to the other boy. Now the girl chimes, "What's the matter, limp-along, can't you catch?"

I rush to Elisabeth's aid, but Nicanor arrives before me. He grabs each boy by the arm. "What brave young men to pick on a little girl, and a lame one at that! Would you please apologize to my friend, or would you prefer that I escort you to your parents?"

The boys' decision is quickly reached. Their regret is mumbled and the bowl is placed in Elisabeth's waiting hands. We stifle our chuckles until the boys and girl have vanished from view.

The Greek smiles at the upturned face of Elisabeth. Carefully she sets the dish down, all the while gazing with adoration at her defender. Her small hands wrap around the dark hairy fingers of Nicanor. Her speechlessness is short lived.

"Hannah-Marah, did you see what he did? I thought only my daddy could be so brave. What if the bowl had been broken? Oh, Shua would've yelled at me." She pauses, then kisses his thumb.

Nicanor puts the child's hand into mine, then cups our hands with his own. I am touched by the nobility of his deed, by the warmth of his grasp, by his nearness.

"Marah! The animal shed is out of fresh straw, please attend to it immediately! Marah, the inn's porch hasn't been swept this afternoon! Marah, fill the lamps ... Marah, come here ... go there!"

If I wasn't so tired I think I would go mad. Shua hovers over my every move, spitting out orders, demanding speed, expecting more than my strength and wit can accomplish.

I am so weary from my labors for this woman that I have little energy left for Elisabeth. I snap at her without provocation. Of late the inn rarely has extra bread. My meager pay cannot feed and clothe us. I see only a future of increasing poverty.

Nicanor is our one haven. His cheerful nature is nourishment for my starving heart. If it weren't for him I don't know what Elisabeth would do. He sees to it that she has at least some occasional fun.

Today I tell him, "Don't ruin the good times we have by asking me such a question."

"Pretty Marah, I'm not trying to destroy our relationship, only improve it. Now be a nice person and marry me."

I laugh and tell him to be on his way. Nicanor, I learn, isn't joking. In his search for a new life he has decided that Elisabeth and I are its beginnings.

I can't think seriously about another marriage. I married Caleb in innocence born from memory loss. Now with full recollection I see again Heber. Heber, ever present in my life with Joel, would surely be present in any marriage. He is yet my lawful spouse. I abandoned him, but my guilt clings as a shadow, never leaving, merely varying in size.

No, I cannot think of marrying again.

"Marah, how many times must I tell you not to let that child in here? A crippled youngster is not a pleasure to our guests!"

Shua dramatically waves her arms and glares at the little girl and her foot. I start to speak in Elisabeth's defense.

"Don't argue! I pay you to serve the inn. Now get her out!"

Elisabeth bravely holds back the portending tears. "I'm leaving," she softly reports.

Daily Shua adds to my duties. I can't do enough to satisfy her. It is as though I embody all that burdens her. Am I to daily labor to exhaustion? Must Elisabeth live with Shua's insults? Are we always to be on the edge of hunger? There must be some way out of this dreadful routine.

There is, if only my conscience hushes.

"Are you positive that you want to marry Nicanor?"

When Elisabeth first asked me, I had assured her that this charming Greek was a man of good humor and at the very least would free me from Shua's rule.

Today, in spite of our new home and full cupboards, her question haunts me. In the beginning weeks of this marriage I believed Nicanor's words, "I only drink to celebrate that at last I have a wife and child. Come, my love, share the wine."

But last night.

"Nicanor," I keep my voice low, "last night you were drunk." He blinks his eyes at me as though trying to remember. I continue, "You said dreadful things both to Elisabeth and to me."

My husband runs his hands over his dark hair. his face is pained. "I'm so sorry. Oh, Marah, I am so very sorry. Please forgive me."

"Perhaps you could be moderate in your drinking." Nicanor grins his appealing boyish grin. "You're absolutely right. Moderation it will be!" Reaching for my arms, he beseeches, "Come here, sweet wife, and let me be intoxicated on your love alone."

The fallen infant bird peers out from the cave of Elisabeth's fist. She mixes meal into a thin mush, and, drop by drop, administers the nourishment. It takes little coaxing for Nicanor to join in the dedicated task of bringing this bird to full feather.

"The narrow sticks are the right size," decides Nicanor. Before my skeptical eyes, this clever man fashions a bird cage, complete with perch. Elisabeth happily transfers the fledgling from the basket to his new home. Several weeks of faithful care will produce a thriving bird.

"Little one," Nicanor turns to Elisabeth following our supper, "it is time to consider where to release the bird."

"What do you mean, 'to release the bird'?"

"You've done an outstanding job nurturing him, now you must do the harder part and let him go."

Elisabeth jumps to her feet and heads for the cage. "He's mine. I won't let him leave!"

Nicanor tells her gently, brushing leaves from his tunic, "Elisabeth, nobody owns anybody. Even if you keep him, every impulse of the bird will be calling him to freedom. Don't you care enough for this little creature to let him fly the skies as he was meant to do?"

Elisabeth glides her hand over the cage. The bird chirps, expecting food.

"Do you think I should let him loose, Hannah-Marah?"

"He is a wild bird and meant to be free."

She limps to Nicanor. "If I let him go, it must be in the prettiest of all places for a bird to live. Do you know of such a spot?"

My husband is fastidious about his person. Traces of supper honey still stick to Elisabeth's face and fingers, yet Nicanor lifts the girl into his arms, endangering his neatness. "I know of such a place. Any bird would be pleased to live there. Tomorrow we'll take him to the site and watch as he heads for the tallest tree."

Nicanor is a choice man. If only he didn't find occasion to lose himself in strong drink.

I am preparing the supper stew when Elisabeth silently moves to my side. She is out of breath and I see tears smeared across her cheeks.

"What is it, child?"

"He's over on the next street." The sobs shake her small frame.

"Who? Tell me, who?"

I hold her until she is able to speak coherently.

"Nicanor. I saw him staggering all over the

197

road. I ran to help him. He slapped me, Hannah-Marah, Nicanor slapped me and said I was ugly!" Again she loses control.

If only an illness or an injury accounted for his behavior, but I suspect otherwise.

"He is drunk?"

Elisabeth rubs her nose. "He is."

Before I hurry from the house I explain to the girl the next steps in stew making.

I find Nicanor sprawled over a low rock fence just off from the road. It takes some doing, but I get him to his feet and home.

He sleeps until the next day. When sobriety returns he is mournful for the episode.

"I'm sorry," Nicanor cries into his trembling hands.

"Why, Nicanor, why?"

"I have a thirst, Marah, such a thirst."

"And only wine can appease it?"

He shakes his head, "I've found nothing else."

This is a good man, quick to laugh, tender and thoughtful. What happens with his mind and to his body when the flask is emptied of wine and he is filled? Is he unaware of what he becomes when drunken? Does his love for us and even himself dissolve in the strong drink? Is there anything I can do to help him?

I own no answers, I simply stroke his head and weep with him.

Our purse, once so full, is losing its fatness. I mention this to Nicanor. "It's my money. I can do with it as I please." Of late I see a harshness about him, whether he is drinking or not. Rather than turn into a total nag, I begin to sew for others. This provides a few extra coins.

I am not imagining things, our household articles are vanishing. I can't blame Elisabeth's forgetting things for these losses. What could be happening to the items? What if the coins I've earned also disappear? How secure are they hidden away in my sewing basket? If they are lost I cannot buy food.

Behind our house grows a young Sycamore. In the bend of one root is a small hollow. I wrap a cloth tightly about my money and push it far into the opening. A rock and dried grasses conceal the secret.

It is at the marketplace that I learn the disgusting solution to the mysterious passing of our possessions. Nicanor sells them in order to keep himself supplied with wine. I learn, too, that it isn't just wine for himself he buys. He invites others, any others, to drink with him. Gossips further tell me that cheers erupt whenever Nicanor walks into the inn.

The day is hot, not even a breeze moves the air, when Shua surprises me with a noon visit.

"I know we've not been friends, Marah. I am uncertain why I even come."

I invite her in.

"I try to run an orderly establishment."

"Yes, I remember."

Shua rubs the knuckles of one hand against her knee. "I wish you would keep Nicanor from my inn. He drinks too much and gets the other guests to join in his rowdiness. I don't like it."

"Have you told him of your feelings?"

Shua's face becomes scarlet and her voice loses its usual force. "I . . . I find it difficult to rebuke him."

"All right, then, I'll tell him your message."

This evening, after our meal, I relate Shua's words.

"Shua came here?" He roars with delight. "My friends and I share a few laughs, but there is no way we disrupt the inn's business. I'll have to tell Shua that she is pretty. That should calm her down."

It is only days later when Shua again is at my door. I offer her a seat and curiously await her complaint. Shua rubs her hands together. Her voice is thin. "It is your husband. He is providing more than wine for his friends." Shua fidgets with the hem of her coat; the color drains from her face. "Lately Nicanor supplies them and himself with the favors of harlots."

"Are you certain?" I choke.

Shua rises. "Very certain." And she is gone.

My stomach reels. The room spins. I struggle to hold back screams. There must be some mistake. Nicanor drinks, but to entertain harlots? No, Shua saw someone else . . . Nicanor, my husband, caressing . . . no . . . no. . . .

"Hannah-Marah!" She is full of girlish giggles as she bursts into the house. "Have you forgotten that we are to meet the mother of my new friend, Adah, this afternoon?"

Not now! I can't face anyone now!

"Hurry. They are waiting for us."

I wash my face, smooth my hair, and join Elisabeth for the visit.

"Did you like Adah and her mother?" queries Elisabeth as we walk home.

"Yes, they are both very nice."

"You were awfully quiet, Hannah-Marah, do you feel all right?"

"I'm fine, just extra tired, I guess." The child is too young to share my burdens.

It is far into the night when Nicanor silently slips into our bed. He reeks of wine. "It is late, Nicanor."

He belches.

"Are you sober enough to talk?"

"You want to talk?" His words are shaky, almost tearful.

"Shua was here again today."

He doesn't respond for several moments. Then, "Shua? She doesn't like me or my friends." He curls into a ball and quietly whimpers himself to sleep.

Our discussion of Shua's visit will have to wait until morning.

"She said what?"

"Shua reported that you are buying the favors of harlots for yourself and your companions."

"Do you believe such a tale?"

"Not if you tell me it isn't so."

Nicanor's eyes search my face. He rubs his elbows and turns his back to me. The pitch of his voice elevates. "What business of yours is it what I do?"

I elevate my own pitch. "I'm your wife! That's what business of mine it is!"

Nicanor spins about to face me. "On our wedding night you must've been aware that I was not unfamiliar with the procedure." A slight sneer crosses his face. "And you, my pretty lady, made it clear to me that you knew what the marriage bed was all about."

"The *marriage* bed, Nicanor!"

"Oh Marah, come on. I am a man and should be allowed a pleasure or two. Let's not argue about this again." He pats my shoulder and leaves.

Does he regard our relationship so casually? Is not the marriage bed sacred?

And then I see it. I left my lawful husband and slept with other husbands . . . even now I do so. My shadow of guilt looms before me, filling every corner of the room. I am as blameworthy as this man.

Strength rushes from my insides. I collapse onto the nearby chair. "Nicanor," I hear myself weakly cry his name. Only that accusing inner voice responds, "Guilty, Marah, guilty."

"Adah is my best friend." Elisabeth beams, "We talk about everything."

I pick up the comb. "Is that so? And just what is everything?"

Elisabeth snickers into her hands. I realize that if I am to know the "everything" I will have to reach into the secret memories of my own girlhood.

"Hold still, please, and let me comb out these snarls."

The child straightens. "Hannah-Marah, do you ever wish that you had a friend you could talk to about everything, too?"

Elisabeth has aimlessly hurled an arrow which directly finds the spot of my deep need.

"Yes."

"I'm almost ten. I could be your friend."

I secure the braid and give her a quick hug. "Thank you, perhaps someday, but now I must hurry to the house of Rufas and pick up the torn tunic."

During the following days I find a heaviness increasing in my arms and legs. Even to move is burdensome. This cannot be reality. Surely I will soon awaken and be released of all horror.

But the nightmare continues. Never have I felt so alone, so utterly alone. I dip my cup in the water jar. There is not one single person who really knows me. Not even Elisabeth is aware that I now live with my fifth husband. I sip the water. And even if anyone knew me, could he ease my guilt and aloneness? Finished with my drink, I replace the cup.

Nothing ultimately satisfies. Nothing lasts. Not love, not relationships, not security, not even the quenching of thirst.

TWENTY-FIVE

Sitting where I am, facing our guests, I can see out the open doorway and observe the people who pass by. My daughter serves spice cakes to our company, Adah and her mother, Johanna. These are Elisabeth's treats, prepared by her own hands.

"What a clever child you are," compliments Johanna. "You must be the delight of Marah's heart."

"Oh, she is indeed . . . even without her cooking skills." I gesture to include Adah. "Little girls bring delight into every day."

Johanna is a gracious woman. Her bearing and manners point to a noble unbringing; her charm is innate to her person. I am flattered that she desires my friendship.

Adah spreads the dried fiber strands over the floor, then explains her technique of basket weaving. As we marvel over her cunning, I happen to glance outside. My eye catches sight of approaching disaster.

Nicanor shuffles down the walkway, his behavior again the product of strong drink. His clothes are in disarray, his hair wild and windblown. He hollers slurred obscenities. I yearn to vanish.

Elisabeth begins to cry. "Make him go away. Please, please, make him go away!"

My husband staggers to the doorway. Vomit clings to his once-impeccable mustache and beard. His tunic is filthied.

Little Adah stares in shocked disbelief. I grope stupidly for words, any words. Calmly Johanna gathers the basket makings, takes her daughter's hand, and bids me a compassionate good-bye.

"Hannah-Marah, why don't you and I move back to Joppa? We could stay with Tabitha."

I reflect upon our good friend and for a short moment fancy the idea. But I answer, "No, this is our home."

"Nicanor is drunk all the time. He is not at all like he used to be." Elisabeth spreads her fingers as though to enlarge her argument. "I don't like him anymore."

I put my arm around the small frame. "I know, dear, I know."

Elisabeth scowls, "Nicanor doesn't care what his drinking does to us. I think we should leave. I don't want to live like this."

I fold my hands and rest them on the table. "We must hope. Perhaps the Nicanor we respect will be returned to us. The drinking is a burden for all of us, especially to Nicanor. There is little I know to do to stop it. We can only hope that he will rid himself of this. Nicanor is not a foolish man. Surely soon he will decide that life is brighter when viewed with sober eyes."

Elisabeth's young face reflects the uncertainty of these days, causing her to look old. I ache to assure her that all will be well, that sunshine and butterflies and sweet cakes will fill her hours.

"Come over by me, child. Would you like to hear a story about a girl who did run away?"

Elisabeth's face softens as she puffs the cushion for maximum comfort. This lover of tales is ready for any adventure I might invent. My story, however, is not pretend. I begin.

"The girl was loved, wealthy, and indulged."

Right off, Elisabeth interrupts. "Was she pretty?"

"Everyone told her she was, so I suspect she must have been." Pleased with the clarification, Elisabeth again prepares to listen. "One day the girl married a goatherd . . . a *handsome* young man," I quickly add. "Her new husband needed her to help tend his growing flocks. But the girl found goat-watching tiresome and difficult. Her husband was too young and too involved with his animals to understand her growing unhappiness.

"One day a beautiful son was born to them. The goatherd said, 'At last a true partner to assist me with the herds.' The girl said, 'At last someone to love who will love me in return.'

"Then a terrible thing happened. A goat battered the little boy to death. Overwhelmed by this loss, the girl blamed God, her husband, and all goats. Everyday the memory of her lost son tormented her. There was only one thing to do, she decided. Run away. Leave the troubles. She tried to convince herself that she left for the sake of others. But the plain truth was that she left for herself."

What happened to her?"

"She saw new places and met many people, but her sorrow followed, and guilt soon was added to the burden she carried."

I lift Elisabeth's chin with my fingertips. She must understand my lesson. *"The girl learned that a safe fortress cannot be built upon the ruins made from other lives."*

Elisabeth stretches and yawns. "I still think we should go back to Joppa."

Our purse is empty. Nicanor's thirst has seen to that. In order to buy wine he has sold most of our household furnishings. Yesterday he even sold my red cushion. If I did not sew, we would not eat.

The sun is directly overhead when Nicanor finally awakens. He is sober.

"Good morning, Marah, how are you today?"

I do not correct his error concerning the time of day. "I am fine."

He goes directly to the purse and shakes it, listening for the clanking of coins.

"It's empty," I tell him.

"Don't you have another purse?"

"That is the only purse." He knows nothing of my coins hidden in the tree root.

Nicanor's face contorts. He reaches into the bag, searching frantically for an overlooked coin. There is none.

"I know you get money for your sewing. Where is it?" I back away. He frightens me when his eyes narrow. "If there is money enough for food," he points to Elisabeth, who is eating a piece of bread, "there is money for wine!" He reddens, "Can't you see I need to buy a little wine, woman?"

He storms through the house, upturning our two pots, upsetting my sewing basket, and kicking the walls. Outraged, I run after him and accuse, "You used to be charming, even noble. Now look at you! Eagerly bowing to the authority of strong drink. Don't you care what it is doing to you?" Glancing at the crouched Elisabeth, I scream, "And to us?"

Nicanor's neck reddens, he swings around, striking my face, then roars, "Wine is available and there are those who will buy!" He charges from the house.

Elisabeth, witness to this spectacle, finds the basin. Tenderly she bathes my swelling cheek.

"Now, Hannah-Marah, now can we go to Joppa?"

The gray morning sky can hardly announce the advent of day. In the yellow light of the lamp's bright flame, I examine Elisabeth's bent foot. "Last evening I ran into a rock as I was coming home from Adah's. It still hurts." Since Nicanor's scene that afternoon, Adah has not been permitted to visit us. I pour oil on the scrape and

208

massage the injured area. Poor child. How wearisome to have to cope with this deformity.

A sharp rap at the door causes us to start.

Elisabeth jerks her foot from me. "Who could that be?"

"Probably a repentant Nicanor." My husband hasn't been home for three days. I dread the scene that is sure to come.

It is not Nicanor. Our early caller is Shua's brother. Dark circles underline his red eyes.

"May I speak with you, Marah?"

"Of course, please come in."

Shua's brother has been back working at the inn all winter. Shua had mentioned to Nicanor how glad she was to be free of so many responsibilities. But why has her brother come to see me? Is Nicanor guilty of some misdeed? Am I going to have to pay for some broken item?

He rejects the offer to sit. "I will be brief. I bring bad news." Remembering Elisabeth, I suggest, "Perhaps you wish to step outside so the child does not hear."

His burden must be overly heavy, for he ignores my concern for Elisabeth. The man runs jerky fingers through his heavy hair.

"Throughout her life Shua found it hard to be close to people. It was hard for her to even engage in casual conversations. I guess my sister had a loneliness that was greater than I knew." He coughs into his fist. The lines of his face deepen.

"Shua and Nicanor . . . they. . . ." This tall keeper of the inn begins to sob. "She's gone . . . her clothes . . . money. . . ." It is clear that for now he simply cannot talk. I have him sit down. I try to supply the words, the words we both are loathe to form.

"Shua and Nicanor have left for somewhere . . . together?"

He shakes his head that it is so. Then he speaks, "I have no idea where they've gone or if they'll ever return."

He offers his sympathy to us and then we are alone.

"I'm glad," declares Elisabeth, adjusting her shoe tie. "I hope Nicanor never comes back."

Once more I know the emptied cup.

TWENTY-SIX

The conversion is complete. Our home is now a place of business. I sew, I weave, and I mend for others.

Most women perform all sewing needs of their families. However, there are those who, for reason of health, ability, or desire, do not. And men, living alone, are often ignorant of the ways of a needle. These people are my customers.

Elisabeth helps with the simpler stitches and is eager to learn all that I can teach. But after the sun has set we pretend that no shop ever existed here. We are merely home.

Elisabeth holds a pomegranate. The lamplight does magical things to her hair, highlighting first this strand and then that one. She peels the fruit carefully.

"Aren't pomegranates beautiful?" Elisabeth extols. "Each little seed is wrapped in its own package." She considers the fruit almost reverently, then pops a few seeds into her mouth.

"I wish I were as pretty as Adah."

"I think you are very pretty, especially when you smile."

This slender, fragile girl with the lovely hair, this daughter of Caleb and daughter of my own heart, is nearing twelve. I wonder if her twisted foot will hinder her opportunities for marriage. If only there were a way that I could guarantee love and safety for her. If only there were an ointment to straighten bent feet; if only there were a physician to heal the lame.

"Yes, Elisabeth, you are very pretty, especially when you smile."

The two girls are weak from a massive bout with the giggles. Elisabeth and Adah often just look at each other and break out laughing. But this time they are exhausted from some caused merriment. "What on earth happened while I was at the marketplace?" They are off again, overcome with laughter. After I put away the food from my basket I try again. "Whatever gave you such amusement?"

"You should've seen him!"

"Seen who?"

"The man who brought in that tunic." A garment is displayed. It is a dreary pink color and ripped up the side. Hardly a reason for such hilarity.

Adah struts to portray the caller. "*'This tear,'*" she mocks, "*'occurred as I swung down from a tree just now. Can you fix it?'*"

Elisabeth interrupts. "We told him it couldn't

be mended with him still in it, so he yanked it off, picked up your gray shawl, and draped it around his waist. *'I'll be back tomorrow,'* he said, and he left. Can you imagine the sight of him walking through town?"

The girls grab towels; similarly wrapped, they strut about the room, then drop with laughter.

I'm not that amused, for the tear is quite extensive. "Since you've committed me to this task, my dear daughter, I suggest that you prepare an exceptional supper for me while I mend."

Elisabeth is with Adah for a morning stroll when the tunic's owner arrives. No wonder the girls laughed so. Absolutely nothing about this man is consistent. His frame is slight while large muscled arms and legs protrude from his short, faded red tunic. An abundant mass of red hair tops his head. His beard is red also, but a different red from his hair. His nost dips downward while his wide mouth edges upward. Heavy dark brows shade his soft gray eyes, which seem to have been borrowed from a kitten. I feel an urge to protect him.

As the man enters, I notice that the faded crimson tunic he wears is a similar hue to the garment I've just mended. Could it be that he laundered the two in the same vat? That certainly could explain the unusual pink of the tunic I mended.

"Have you finished the sewing?" His voice, deep and resonant, doesn't fit him either.

"I have."

He examines the seam in the light from the

doorway. "You did a fine piece of mending." His eyes shift from the garment to take in the room's contents, which are certainly few. "Would you like me to pay you with money or pottery?"

"Since I can't eat pottery, I prefer money." I tell him the price of my work.

"Then I'll have to come back." He picks up his tunic and starts to leave. I jump to the door and pull the garment from him. He shakes his hands as though I had injured him. This red-haired man resembles a kitten even more than before. My urge to protect him, however, vanishes. It is difficult enough for a woman alone to make a living without some person trying to cheat her.

My hair is brushed and braided for the night. Elisabeth notes that the oil in the lamp is almost gone. We decide to let the lamp extinguish itself. Tomorrow we will buy a new supply. The hush of night gathers us into its quiet. I pray for sleep to claim me, sparing me from the loneliness that torments my heart. Nicanor has been gone nearly two years. I miss him and wish that I didn't. I wonder if he and Shua are still together, and if he is yet bound to strong drink.

We oversleep. Already people pass our house. Elisabeth scurries about with our breakfast preparations. I lift out our wash water and pour it over our stone pathway. A clean path invites customers.

After breakfast we take the day's mending outside. The sunlight makes for more perfect work. My needle, moving in and out of the fabric, seems to be an extension of my hand. I cannot complain, for without this work Elisabeth and I would be destitute.

Puzzled as to why a shadow crosses my lap, I see that the red-haired man has returned. He raises his hand and meekly waves. "I have your money."

"Fine. I'll get your tunic."

He offers my wage in a small, lovely bowl. The shy smile improves his features. "The dish is an apology for the delay." He hands me the gift. "I am Beno of Sychar, student of Jabesh the potter. These past three months I've been studying his advanced ways with clay." Boldly he adds, "If you ever need new vessels, I recommend his wares."

We scarcely have enough to buy food and oil. When could I ever buy new pottery? Just the same, I comment on the beauty of the new dish and thank him. Then I remember, "The girls said that you have my gray shawl. Would you return it soon, please."

"What news do you bring back from the well, Hannah-Marah?" I set the water jar in its customary corner. Elisabeth savors every morsel of gossip I glean. "Rome is sending a new procurator to Caesarea. The crops should provide a good harvest. Martha's baby is overdue and," I turn away and whisper, "Adah may have an admirer."

Elisabeth gasps. "That must be the secret she said she had! Did you learn who it is?"

"No, Johanna just said that a young man has been a frequent visitor of late."

The girl bites her lip and reviews every prospect she can imagine. "Oh, I wish I knew, I wish I knew."

Elisabeth is absolutely no help in dinner preparations. Nor does she notice that someone raps at our door.

A Roman soldier, angular and expressionless, peers down his stolid cheeks. "Are you the woman who sews?"

"I am."

"The edge of my cloak has frayed. I wish it repaired."

My animosity toward Rome lurches through me. Some people wear rags, and gratefully so. Yet here stands this deputy of Caesar complaining of a frayed hem. The mending, of course, will be done; the soldier, naturally, will pay; but the money undoubtedly will come from the taxing of my countrymen.

"Have this done by tomorrow afternoon." He doesn't ask if it is convenient, just, "have it done." Typical of Rome.

Elisabeth, momentarily forgetting Adah's caller, watches the stiff-shouldered man march down the street. "Will Rome forever be bossing us, Hannah-Marah? Because if it will, then I think I shall marry a soldier. Did you see how handsome he was?"

I cannot take her comment lightly. "Elisabeth, Rome intends to rule the entire world for all time. But always there will be brave men and women who resist tyranny." I consider again the cave and the faces of Joel, Abigail, Sweeper. Returning to the subject of Elisabeth's future husband, I advise, "I think you could find a better choice for marriage than a tool of Rome. After all, carpenters, farmers, and potters also produce nice looking men."

Elisabeth arches her eyebrows. *"Potters?"*

Remembering Beno, I quickly add, "Landowners, teachers, tanners. . . ."

TWENTY-SEVEN

Two days later Beno returns my shawl. I thank him. The following day he comes with a tear in his crimson tunic. I stitch it. The next day he has a long rip in his coat. I repair it. Next he has split his undergarment. I fix that also. This morning he comes wanting to sell me pottery. I don't believe it.

"You know I can't afford dishes!"

Beno grins, arranges the bowls just inside my door, tilts his head to one side, and beguiles me. "Can you afford time to talk with me?" I wish this man would stop looking so appealing.

Beno stacks our two cushions on the low stool. From this vantage he relates his life's history. I learn that his family owns vineyards. Since their father's death four years ago, Beno and his brothers have shared the responsibilities and revenues.

"I am a widower."

Before I learn more, Elisabeth and Adah burst in upon us. "Is it all right if I eat lunch with Adah? Her grandmother made a stew."

"Yes, but be home by mid-afternoon. This jacket needs to be delivered."

I give Beno lunch, thinking he will leave after he has eaten. The food only strengthens him. I am not sure why he chooses to share all these events with me. Perhaps he is lonely. He did say he was a widower. I know how it feels to be alone.

"My sweet wife, Sarah, died of the fever." His usually deep voice shrinks in the telling. "We were married but a short time, not even a year."

I look up from my stitching, "How long ago was that?"

"Over two years now. Sometimes even yet at night I reach over to touch her. . . ." He doesn't finish his sentence.

I put aside my sewing and focus on this man with the mellow eyes, the kitten eyes. "I'm sorry. Death is harsh. Its sting is inescapable."

Beno clears his throat. "I couldn't work after Sarah died. I didn't care about vineyards, or eating, or anything. My family worried that I'd grieve myself to death. To lead me from this depression my brothers took turns taking me to distant places.

"It was at the coast of the Great Sea that life returned to me. I can't explain it," Beno rubs his thumbs together, "but the sea gave back my life."

Peculiar. The sea robs and the sea gives.

Beno rises and steps away from me. Then,

swinging around, he smiles, his mouth forming a broad crescent. "When I was a boy I often imagined myself a potter. It was at the beach, as I molded the sands, that the dream rused back. *I really could be a potter!*

"My brothers were relieved that I had found a reason to live. 'Go study under Jabesh,' they advised. 'Learn to be the best potter ever.' So I came to Sebaste to study Jabesh's advanced techniques and skills."

Beno bows and apologizes, "I've talked far too long. Thank you for listening to me. You are not only a lovely woman, you are kind."

Gradually our home fills with Beno's handiwork. I appreciate the gift of the new dishes, not only for reason of their beauty, but because Nicanor sold most of our pottery to buy wine.

Elisabeth rearranges the cupboard. "Isn't it fun having so many bowls and cups?" She pauses, then faces me fully. "Hannah-Marah, I think Beno likes you."

"I like him, too. Sometimes I even forget how comical he looks."

"No, I mean he LIKES you."

I avoid her eyes and hopefully, her meaning. "What did you and Adah do today?"

Elisabeth won't be outmaneuvered. "We talked about you and Beno. Do you think you'll marry him?"

"I've had enough husbands."

Certainly she knows that. After all, she is mindful of Nicanor, Caleb, and that I was married at the time of the shipwreck. She knows nothing of my other marriages. There is no reason to overwhelm her with my history.

Occasionally I do fret that I might meet someone in Sebaste who remembers me from years ago, someone who recalls Eleazor and Heber. Hopefully the anonymity afforded by this populous city will protect my secrets. Heber will forever be tending goats. I never worry of meeting him in town. I sigh. The only other one who knows of all my marriages is God himself.

This idea of adding yet another husband disturbs me. I intend never to be wife of anyone. As the days pass, Elisabeth plants seeds to the contrary.

"Wouldn't it be helpful to have a man to lift the stones?"

"Doesn't Beno remind you of my daddy?"

"It must be nice to have a husband to grow old with."

She is beginning to irk me with her ploys.

As the days pass I find that I am peeved with everyone and everything. I sew with a madness. I cook with a vengeance. If the neighbor's rooster doesn't quiet down, I think I might step on him.

"Good morning," cheers a smiling Beno. "And how is my favorite seamstress today?"

"Just fine," I retort.

Beno tucks his thumbs in his armpits and boasts, "Jabesh says that I may surpass even his skills. I am nearly through with my studies here in Sebaste."

"That's nice," I lie. I don't want him to leave.

Beno gently shakes my shoulders. "No, it isn't.

It means that soon I'll be returning to Sychar. I don't like the thought of not seeing you."

Gladness gallops through me. He feels the same about me!

But where can it lead? At once my frustrations pounce back. I am angry for allowing that moment of gladness.

Beno suddenly drops to one knee and lifts his hands to me. "Please listen to my pitiful plight. You know the dreadful state of my clothes, *always* getting torn and all. I need a seamstress to *always* be nearby." He wipes his nose with the heel of his hand. His face sobers. "Marah, I cannot return to Sychar without you. Please marry me. See how much I need you," his eyes twinkle, "how much my clothes need you?"

How dare he make sport of me! Who does he think he is to offer such a flippant proposal?

"If you are asking me to be your wife, the answer is no!"

"But, I can't leave you! Come with me to Sychar."

I glare at him. "No!"

"Buy, why?"

The nerve of this man. I don't owe him explanations or reasons or. . . .

"Because you are careless with your clothes, are loud, unsettled," now that I have started, the words keep coming, "immature, talkative, unsophisticated, and . . . *red-haired!*"

He stands doggedly in my doorway, then dips his chin, directing his gray kitten-eyes upward. "But, Marah! I really do love you. I want to marry you!"

"Please, Beno, go!"

The man doesn't budge, rather he sprawls his arms and legs across my doorway. "Not until you consent to be my wife!"

My exasperation enlarges into fury. I grab a bowl, a new gift from Beno, and hurl it at this person responsible for my rage. My aim is dreadful. The dish completely misses Beno and crashes upon the top edge of my large water jar. We stand mute as the rim of the jar shatters, while Beno's carefully crafted bowl spins, unbroken, across the room, wobbles, then stills.

Beno kisses the top of my head, "I'll be back, Marah."

I pick up the bowl and cry. I sweep up the broken fragments of my water jar and cry more. I drop to my bench and weep into my hands.

Where? Where? Where is that tree which was to sweeten life's bitter pool? Will I ever find that for which I so urgently thirst?

Despondent, I lift my needle and watch the in and out rhythmic movement upon the cloth. Marah, Marah, bitter water. Marah, Marah. . . .

TWENTY-EIGHT

"Beno hasn't been here all week. How come?"

"Perhaps these have been unnatural days for him and he hasn't ripped anything."

Elisabeth half laughs. "I miss him. He cheered me up with his funny ways." She shakes out her coat. "Have you seen my shell necklace?"

"No, dear, when did you last have it?"

"Yesterday, at the market . . . I think." Elisabeth searches the cupboard, wiggling each dish, listening for a rattle indicating the lost necklace is found.

Poor Elisabeth, she would forget her ears if they weren't attached to her head. Once more I dutifully give her my speech concerning taking care of one's possessions.

". . . there is nothing so interesting, so world moving, so marvelous that you should lose responsibility over your possessions!"

"But Hannah . . . ."

"You heard me, Elisabeth!" The trembling of her lower lip causes me to find a softer tone. "I'll tell you what. If ever I find something so interesting, so world moving, so marvelous that I am caused to lose or to forget a possession in my responsibility, I promise that I won't scold you for losing things for six months."

We laugh and hug each other. "I might have left my necklace at Adah's. Today, when I go there, I'll see if she found it."

After Elisabeth leaves I start to recheck the cupboard when a feeble rap at the door interrupts my search.

Beno stands before me. His clothes are in shreds. "See," he accuses, "see how I need a seamstress to be by my side at all times? How can you turn me away?"

"Beno, I'm not. I just won't marry you." I have to laugh. "Whatever have you done to your clothes?"

"Actually these aren't mine. Jabesh has a huge bushel of rags. I borrowed these to emphasize my plight, to soften your hard heart. Now, may I come in?"

"If you promise that you won't ask me to marry you."

"Agreed, but first. . . ." He runs to the outside corner of my house returning with a large item covered with a long cloth. "Here, this is for you."

Under the wrap I find the most beautiful water jar I have ever beheld. The shape, the painting, the smooth texture. . . . "Oh, Beno, it is lovely."

"If it weren't for me your other jar would yet be whole."

I am overwhelmed and ashamed. "Beno, I'm sorry for that outburst. It wasn't even you that brought it forth. It's just that, well, you know that Elisabeth's father drowned and Nicanor left me. It is hard for me to live alone, Beno. But it is harder for me to consider another marriage."

Beno takes my hand. "Yes, I know. And I realize that your ties with Nicanor haven't come to a lawful end. But I can't bear to leave Sebaste without you."

Perhaps I should tell him of the whole of my past. Would he then be interested in me?

He seems to know my thoughts. "Marah, it doesn't matter to me that you have had other husbands, or even now are another's. I want you. More than breath, I need you."

Beno lets my hand fall, scratches his beard, clears his throat, and scratches his beard once again. "What I say is with respect, love, and desperation. Please don't let my words insult you." He falls silent and stares at the new water jar.

I don't know what to say so I, too, stare at the jar.

"What if . . . Marah, what if we didn't bother with the sanction of a ceremony? What if you just came to Sychar with me? Everyone would simply assume that I'd married a widow with a daughter. We needn't say otherwise."

I am shocked at the audacity of his plan.

"What about Elisabeth? What would such an arrangement do to her?"

Beno pulls at his red beard. "I suppose we would try to protect her and not let her know we've skipped legalities."

I shake my head. I can't speak. I know he presents this plan not to dishonor us, but to provide a solution.

"Whatever I have to do, Marah, to have you with me, I'll do. I promise to protect you and to support you." He nears until our faces almost touch. For the first time he takes me into his arms. His warm, moist kiss lingers until I well-nigh faint with desire for him. Beno holds me for a long while, smiles into my soul, and finally backs away. He pauses at the door, lifts one hand, and waves good-bye.

What am I to do? Whatever am I to do? Is it possible that we could keep such a relationship secret? What sort of a town is Sychar? Half smiling, I wonder if any of the people there are as odd as Beno?

Never have I felt so confused and unable to think. Perhaps a walk about the marketplace will clear my mind. Somehow I need to find wisdom and direction.

The mid-afternoon sun has conquered the sky—I scan it, horizon to horizon. Not a cloud challenges this bright victor. The air is warm and lightly scented with new blooms.

I am further cheered by the usual bustle of shoppers and shouts from eager sellers. Surely soon I will know what to do about Beno.

Many tubs of produce prove the land's fertility. As I reach to examine the grapes, I am bumped from behind. The offender is a small boy, perhaps no more than five.

"I'm sorry, lady. I was trying to reach that basket. I didn't mean to bump you."

As I start to speak forgiveness, my mouth locks open. A bizarre mixture of anguish and unspeakable joy silences me. The dark curls, the wide-set eyes . . . Aaron! Of course it cannot be, yet I stand transfixed, unable to move or talk.

"I said I was sorry, lady."

I hear myself explain, "You're forgiven, my young friend. I was caught by surprise at how much you look like a little boy I once knew."

"Probably my brother, Aaron. Grandma Anna says I look just like him."

In spite of the sun's warm presence, I shiver. *Aaron? Grandma Anna?*

"Is your grandma with you?"

"No, she's home with Grandpa. He hurt his back. I came here with my parents." He points to a man and woman several shops away.

I pull my headpiece across my face. Thus hidden I stare at the pair.

It really is Heber. He is heavier now, and in full beard. The woman carries a crying infant. Heber takes the baby from her arms and in moments soothes the child into smiles. In disbelief I watch as Heber coos at the small face, then kisses the woman's brow. Not a goat is in sight.

"I have a new brother again."

"You have other brothers?"

"Yes, lady, I do. One older, one younger, and

that new brother, too. If Aaron weren't dead we'd be five brothers. But," he adds, "Aaron had a different mother."

"Oh?"

"I think she died or something. Father and Grandpa won't ever talk about her. Grandma Anna will. Once she even showed me a pretty box and said it had belonged to Aaron's mother. I have to go. Are you sure I didn't hurt you?"

The dark eyes bind my heart. The soft curls touch buried memories. I lift my arms. "Maybe I'd better have a hug just to make certain."

The little boy wraps his chubby arms about me. I hold him. No, it is Aaron I embrace.

Before I can utter a word, the child bounds away to join his parents.

From the privacy of my veiled view I watch Heber greet Aaron's look-alike. The little boy takes his mother's hand, while Heber shifts the baby to one arm and joins hands with the woman.

My presence in Sebaste is a threat to this family, to this small boy with the dark curls. I wipe at my eyes, expecting the bitter tears. Instead I find that all my springs, all my wells, and all my cisterns have dried.

I turn and walk away.

TWENTY-NINE

>>)((((

"It *is* Beno! It *is* Beno!"

This bulletin, shouted and reshouted, brings a small mob upon us. Surely the whole of Sychar is populated with friends of Beno. Amidst back slapping, kisses, tears, and cheers he is welcomed home.

A lanky man calls attention to Elisabeth and me. "Look! Beno has brought back a wife and an almost-grown child."

Beno lifts my hand. "This is Marah, a beautiful widow I met while in Sebaste. She is a seamstress."

The crowd roars its hilarity. Beno's past must include many torn clothes. Turning to Elisabeth, he adds, "Meet Marah's daughter, Elisabeth. She now is also my daughter."

Elisabeth gratefully smiles at Beno. Guilt again twists my heart. Elisabeth believes that Beno and I have made our union lawful.

We are besieged at once with back slapping, kisses, tears, and cheers. Elisabeth and I are welcomed home.

Sychar is not a city like Sebaste or Caesarea. There are no armies of Rome stationed here, no great buildings or theaters, no colonnaded streets. However, it is the noisiest place I have lived. People don't seem to live in their houses, rather activities are done outdoors: cooking, eating, laundry, spinning. Even babies nap upon the ground. It is as though nobody wants to miss a single thing that is happening to anybody. Or do I imagine all this, living as I do in continual fear that our secret sin will be uncovered?

In the evenings, after supper, the men gather at the town's center to swap tales, news, and opinions. This is typical of all Palestine; what isn't typical is that I, a woman, am invited to join this night's session to tell about Joppa.

All day I fight uneasiness. Do these men only pretend to honor me as Beno's wife? Do they suspect the truth of our adulterous relationship? I recall that according to Moses a stoning is in order. These are fairly religious people.

"Maybe I should stay home, Beno."

"You've been praised by this invitation. And deservedly so. You must come."

"But women don't attend such doings, and I am a woman."

"The townsmen know that." He smiles coyly. "They also know that you are a woman of learning. You lived in Joppa. Many of these men have never been to the coast. They relish news of other cities. Relax, you'll be among friends."

231

And family. Beno's ever-widening circle of family join with the men for the evening event. True to Beno's words, I find a kind and respectful audience. I tell of Joppa; once the lone harbor of Palestine, now struggling to survive the mighty competition of Caesarea.

It is late when Beno's oldest brother concludes the session. He thanks me, commenting, "You said things, Marah, with such clarity that I feel as if I've actually been to Joppa tonight." The others speak out their concurrence.

Beno and I walk home in the night illumined by a starry heaven.

"You made me proud." Beno squeezes me. "You'll have to participate another time."

I shake my head no. "My knees trembled and my insides churned the entire time. I don't think I'll join the session ever again!"

"Not even if you happen to remember some exciting event that occurred to you in Joppa?"

"Not even then," I tell him.

"What if tomorrow or next week some marvelous thing befalls you . . . you'd want to share that with the townsmen, wouldn't you?" He kisses my cheek. "But you have to tell me first."

I love this red-haired man. "Beno, if anything outstandingly wonderful ever comes across my path, I'll run first to you, then to all the men in the village."

"Agreed. Me first, then the others."

We laughingly speculate on what exciting thing will happen to me tomorrow or next week.

"I like Sychar. Your family and friends have been gracious to Elisabeth and to me. This night, in spite of my apprehensions, has been one of the best evenings of my life."

Beno's hand on my waist pulls me closer to his side. His low whisper stirs my desires. "It will be even better when we get home."

Beno never mentions marriage, but I know he wishes our union were lawful. I find pleasure in our embrace. Perhaps it is that the pleasure is unauthorized, and in my search for "the tree which sweetens," I look even in forbidden areas.

As we hasten our pace, Beno observes, "I'm glad you like my town, even with its many lacks." I start to protest that his town lacks nothing, but he shushes me and laughingly concludes, "At least you'll have to admit that no one of any importance will ever bother to come to Sychar."

Elisabeth is happy to be caretaker of Beno's twin four-year-old nephews this week. The boys, who adore Elisabeth, are delighted to be in her charge. Their mother, busy with a new daughter, is just short of ecstatic with the arrangement. I, on the other hand, remember pleasanter times with goats running loose in the house.

This morning both Elisabeth and I take the boys to Beno's nearby shop. The twins squeal as Beno slams and punches the clay, ridding it of unwanted bubbles. The children gasp their wonder as they watch the shapeless mass on the potter's wheel become a lovely bowl. For several moments the boys are actually quiet as Beno explains the use of paddles, scrapers, and kilns. Then they grow bored with the potter and his work.

As we approach our house, Elisabeth asks, "Can the boys play inside for awhile?" The little ones smile sweetly at me.

"Of course," I say, moving to the cupboard to prepare them a treat. It is a hot day and our home offers a little coolness.

"Stop!" screams Elisabeth. I jerk around in time to see my sewing fly across the room. I race to retrieve spools of thread and half-finished garments. Elisabeth wails her regret. The boys back up against the far wall, their lower lips quivering in unison. Large frightened eyes join Elisabeth's supplication in a plea for mercy. To my surprise, I give it, but with the warning that my sewing baskets must never, never be neared.

As they snack, I go outside to grind the wheat into flour, hoping to release my frustrations productively. It is only mid-morning. How am I to last the day, the week, with these wild ones about?

The shadows shorten. I look up and wonder what power propels the sun on its daily arc across the sky. I have so many questions that play about in my mind, so many ponderings that trouble my soul.

"Hannah-Marah! Hannah-Marah!" It is Elisabeth again. In spite of the urgency of her voice, I, with slow deliberation, set aside my grain, flour, and grinding bowl. The boys have probably upturned the cupboards. I must send them outside for the rest of the day.

The twins stand side by side on a bench. Elisabeth points to the damage. They have knocked over the water jar, spilling the precious contents all over the floor. Elisabeth has righted the jar and attempted to mop up the flow.

"Is there any water left?" I ask.

Elisabeth shakes the jar. "Not much, maybe a cup or two. Oh, I am so sorry. We were playing wolf and sheep. Before I knew it, these two sheep charged right into the jar."

We cannot do without water until evening. The children will be thirsty and Beno needs water for his work. "Do you want me to go to the well, Hannah-Marah?"

That would mean a long walk in the noon heat for this crippled girl. It would also mean that I'd be watching the twins.

"No, Elisabeth, I will go."

I pour the remaining water into a bowl and head for Jacob's well.

The sun is hot and the road is dusty. The empty jar sits lightly upon my head. How like my life is this water jar. Full. Empty. Full. Empty. Is this how life is always to be? Is there no permanent filling? Is there no drink to satisfy my soul's great thirst?

Jacob's well holds cool water. I am at least grateful for that. And I am glad that no one draws at midday, for I am really not in a mood for chatter.

But I see someone is already at the well. A young man sits facing me. I feel he has been expecting me.

Now he [Jesus] had to go through Samaria. So he came to a town in Samaria called Sychar, near the plot of ground Jacob had given to his son Joseph. Jacob's well was there, and Jesus, tired as he was from the journey, sat down by the well. It was about the sixth hour.

When a Samaritan woman came to draw water, Jesus said to her, "Will you give me a drink?" (His disciples had gone into the town to buy food.)

The Samaritan woman said to him, "You are a Jew and I am a Samaritan woman. How can you ask me for a drink?" (For Jews do not associate with Samaritans.)

Jesus answered her, "If you knew the gift of God and who it is that asks you for a drink, you would have asked him and he would have given you living water."

"Sir," the woman said, "you have nothing to draw with and the well is deep. Where can you get this living water? Are you greater than our father Jacob, who gave us the well and drank from it himself, as did also his sons and his flocks and herds?"

Jesus answered, "Everyone who drinks this water will be thirsty again, but whoever drinks the water I give him will never thirst. Indeed, the water I give him will become in him a spring of water welling up to eternal life."

The woman said to him, "Sir, give me this water so that I won't get thirsty and have to keep coming here to draw water."

He told her, "Go, call your husband and come back."

"I have no husband," she replied.

Jesus said to her, "You are right when you say you have no husband. The fact is, you have had five husbands, and the man you now have is not your husband. What you have just said is quite true."

"Sir," the woman said, "I can see that you are a prophet. Our fathers worshiped on this mountain, but you Jews claim that the place where we must worship is in Jerusalem."

Jesus declared, "Believe me, woman, a time is coming when you will worship the Father neither on this mountain nor in Jerusalem. You Samaritans worship what you do not know; we worship what we do know, for salvation is from the Jews. Yet a time is coming and has now come when the true worshipers will worship the Father in spirit and truth, for they are the kind of worshipers the Father seeks. God is spirit, and his worshipers must worship in spirit and in truth."

The woman said, "I know that Messiah" (called Christ) "is coming. When he comes, he will explain everything to us."

Then Jesus declared, "I who speak to you am he."

Just then his disciples returned and were surprised to find him talking with a woman. But no one asked, "What do you want?" or "Why are you talking with her?"

Then, leaving her water jar, the woman went back to the town and said to the people, "Come, see a man who told me everything I ever did. Could this be the Christ?" They came out of the town and made their way toward him.

Many of the Samaritans from that town believed in him because of the woman's testimony, "He told me everything I ever did." So when the Samaritans came to him, they urged him to stay with them, and he stayed two days. And because of his words many more became believers.

They said to the woman, "We no longer believe just because of what you said; now we have heard for ourselves, and we know that this man really is the Savior of the world."

John 4:4–30, 39–42 (NIV)

BIBLIOGRAPHY

A Commentary on the Holy Bible. New York:
The Macmillan Co., 1955.

A Standard Bible Dictionary. New York, London:
Funk & Wagnalls Company, 1909.

Commentary on the Holy Scriptures, vol. *John,*
J. P. Lange. Grand Rapids: Zondervan Publishing House,
1871.

Great People of the Bible and How They Lived. New York,
Montreal, London, Sydney: The Reader's Digest
Association, Inc., 1974.

Matthew Henry's Commentary on the Whole Bible, vol. *V.*
London, Edinburgh: Fleming H. Revell Company, 1721.

Rand McNally Bible Atlas, E. G. Kraeling. New York,
Chicago, San Francisco: Rand McNally, 1956.

The Bible Almanac, J. I. Packer, M. C. Tenney, W. White,
Jr. Nashville: Thomas Nelson Publishers, 1980.

The Book of Knowledge, vol. 4. New York: The Groiler
Society Inc., 1957.

The Encyclopedia Americana, vol. 12 and 23. New York,
Chicago, Washington, D.C.: Americana Corporation,
1958.

The Interpreter's Dictionary of the Bible, vol. A-D.
Nashville, New York: Abingdon Press, 1962.

The Interpreter's One-Volume Commentary on the Bible.
Nashville, New York: Abingdon Press, 1971.

The Life and Times of Jesus the Messiah, vol. 1,
A. E. Edersheim. Grand Rapids: William B. Eerdmans
Publishing Co., 1956.

The Twentieth Century Bible Commentary. New York:
Harper Brothers Publishers, 1955.